Mooncalf

Linda L. Zern

This is a work of fiction. Names, characters, places, and incidents either are the product of the author's imagination or are used fictitiously, and any resemblance to actual persons, living or dead, business establishments, events, or locales is entirely coincidental.

DEDICATION

"Graft in the branches . . . both old and young . . . that all may be nourished once again for the last time." (Jacob 5:63)

ACKNOWLEDGMENTS

For the keepers, readers, makers, polishers, and fixers of the stories, thank you for helping me with mine. Always and forever you make me glad to be a storyteller— Sherwood, Sarah, Heather, Maren, Marie, Jeanette, Becky . . .

Mostly, I want to thank the children who remind me that loving is as easy as holding someone's hand.

Mooncalf: (Noun) (1) A foolish, gullible, overly trusting person (2) A person, esp. a youth, who spends time mooning about (3) monstrous.

1. Before

When the world was new and orange trees grew wild, which is to say that the trees grew here or there or wherever and not in neat, straight lines the way people like to grow trees now, the people grew wild too, teaching their children the right ways to live and be happy. Those people taught their children that the tree of life was really an orange tree that lived forever—the same way everyone lives forever, even after they die. That's the way the people and the trees used to be.

They taught their children that when people died they went to live in a beautiful garden with grapes and apples and pomegranates and, of course, oranges. In the garden, they got to play games and be happy. One of the games they played was with the fruit from the orange trees. The people who had been old when they died played with oranges that were dried up and brown. The people who were in the middle of living when they died played with plump round oranges—perfectly ripe. The young ones, the children who died before they had ripened into grown-ups, played with small, green oranges.

When the world was new and orange trees grew wild, the people grew wild too, believing that their children lived forever, even after they died, playing with oranges that were the wrong color.

2. What Leah Thought

Being swallowed alive by a whale would be more fun than this. Pinocchio was lucky.

3. New Girl

The bus engine growled, loud enough to rattle the windows.

"Hey! There's a big, red monkey riding on the roof of that car," a girl sitting behind Leah hollered.

"No, it's a dog—a big, red dog. And it's surfing right up on top of that roof." Across the aisle from Leah, a boy with big horse teeth pointed, screaming with laughter.

"That is so far out and gross!" someone else said.

"Hey, green sweater girl!" One of the big kids in the back of the bus started yelling at one of the little kids sitting in the front of the bus.

Leah was one of the kids sitting in the front of the bus, and she was little.

She did not turn around.

He couldn't be yelling at her, not on her first day at a new school. He's not. It was a mistake. Leah looked down at her green sweater and started to count the pearl buttons. Why couldn't she be a turtle with no ears and disappear inside her green sweater shell? It was probably pretty quiet inside a turtle's shell.

"Look at that! It's right up on the roof of the car." It was another girl's voice, breathless and squeaky. "Right on top of the roof. How does it stay up there? Look. Hey, new girl with the red hair, is that your car?"

It would be fun to look. It really would. It would be so nice to laugh because some big kid in the back of the bus had laughed, and then she'd be like the other kids. Not some girl with no name in a green sweater. Slipping lower and lower in her seat, she listened to the laughing as it got bigger and deeper, as big and as deep as an ocean full of green sea turtles and white pearls that people made into buttons.

Giggles rolled through the bus like a wave. The giggle wave rolled over Leah, making it hard for her to breathe. Her ears felt hot and her hands felt cold, and she couldn't feel her toes at all.

She tipped her head back and pretended that the metal strips on the roof of the bus were the inside bones of a whale. Squishing her eyes almost closed made it easier to imagine being inside a whale's belly like Pinocchio. If she were a sea turtle in a green shell swallowed whole by a whale, it would make sense to have cold hands and numb toes, and if she closed her eyes all the way shut and concentrated, the laughing almost sounded like a whale's tummy rumbling.

Better to be eaten by a whale than to be laughed at on her first day in a new school.

4. What Olympia Thought

Olympia watched the new girl in the green

sweater try to melt into the hard plastic of the bus seat. She knew the girl's name. It was Leah. They were in Mrs. Ward's class together.

In Mrs. Ward's class they sat like the alphabet, *A*s first and then *B*s, followed by *C*s, followed by all the rest of the letters. Olympia Crooms with a *C* sat in the seat behind Leah Breck with a *B*. Olympia wondered if the new girl had noticed her.

Maybe the new girl had been too worried about her first day at Evegan Elementary to notice anybody. Olympia watched the girl, whose name was Leah, sink farther and farther down into the seat as the laughter on the bus got louder and bigger. Soon Olympia could only see the top of the girl's red hair.

"Look at that grossed-out dork dog." First Brian said it, and then all the big kids were chanting it—dork dog, dork dog, dork dog.

Olympia could see that Leah had closed her eyes.

"Brian, be quiet and sit down," said Miss Brinker. At first the bus driver had looked up and frowned into her overhead mirror as the windshield wipers slapped rain back and forth on the windshield, but in the end even Miss Brinker was trying not to laugh.

Olympia needed to see what was making Miss Brinker look like she had a bee trapped inside her mouth. Standing up, she pressed her face to the window and peeked to see between the slow drips of rain.

"Oh no."

Kids tried to shout over the laughing and

chanting. One voice yelled loudest.

"Your mom's almost here to pick you up, new girl, and so is your dog."

5. Old Town Road

Leah could hear the hissing sigh the bus made when Miss Brinker stepped on the brakes. The hissing sound was the sound of a whale whistling through its blowhole, and the engine rumble was the whale breathing. *Being a little fish inside a big fish would feel just like this.* She looked up, counting the whale's rib bones one more time.

The bus stopped at the end of Old Town Road, but the creaky door didn't open, probably because of the rain.

Miss Brinker glanced back at Leah, holding up one finger to let her know it would be another minute before she opened the bus door. It felt like her mom was taking a long, long time to meet the bus.

"What kind of dog is that? Hey you, girl?"

The whale game wasn't working anymore. She couldn't make the yelling go away. She slammed her eyes shut and tried imagining that she only understood whale whistles and turtle whispers. It didn't work.

"Is that your dog, new girl?"

"Her name is Leah."

Her name. Someone knew her name. Someone sitting right next to her, close enough that she could feel an elbow next to her elbow, a knee next to her knee. When had that happened?

Sometimes you miss stuff when you ride around in the belly of a whale all the time, and there might be someone else floating around next to you. It was a surprising, scary idea.

Turning a little bit, she opened her eyes and peeked at the stranger sitting next to her. Smiling, the girl poked her tongue through a gap made by a missing tooth. Smiling back, Leah wiggled her tongue at the girl through an identical space in her own teeth.

The surprising girl reached for Leah's hand.

"My name's Olympia. I'm in your class. I sit right behind you, because I'm a *C* for Crooms, and you're a *B* for Breck."

While she talked about the letters in their names, the girl squeezed Leah's hand until Leah squeezed back, until she couldn't hear what the kids in the back of bus were yelling.

Looking down at their hands, Leah saw a perfect hand-basket, an in and out weaving of light and dark fingers.

Our hands look so pretty together, she thought.

6. Soggy Dog

Olympia could feel how perfectly their hands fit together; it was like holding hands with herself.

Behind them, more and more laughter rattled through the bus.

Outside the bus, car brakes squealed, stopped, and then squealed again. It sounded like a giant squeak toy inching down the road.

Miss Brinker tried to shout louder than the kids who were shouting, the bus driver telling everyone to sit down and to hush up. Nobody did.

"Are they going to make fun of me until I die?" Leah whispered.

Olympia looked over at Leah and tried smiling, but she could only make half her mouth curve up, and she knew it was a bad smile.

"No, next week they'll be back making fun of Tommy Watson for eating paste when he thinks no one is looking." Olympia hesitated, trying to think of something else to say to make her feel better. "Leah? Can I ask you something?"

"What?" Leah shot straight up in her seat.

Olympia peeked over the bus seat at the craziness behind them. All the kids were crowded to one side of the bus, smashing their noses flat against the windows—fingers pointing, hands digging into sides.

"Do you know that dog riding on the top of your car?"

Car brakes squealed, and rubber tires squeaked across asphalt.

The sky outside was dark and heavy and full of winter storm. It rumbled and crackled. Rain tapped away at the metal roof over their heads. It would have been cozy if Miss Brinker didn't look like she was going to knuckle people on the head as soon as she got a chance. Next to Olympia, Leah sat like a statue made of icy white marble, staring straight ahead.

Olympia made her voice soft, leaning forward

so that Leah would be sure to look at her.

"You're going to have to look sometime." Olympia smiled and nodded. "You can do it. It's okay. It's not like the time that my cousin Diane's little sister cut Diane's ponytail off with her Me-Maw's pinking sheers, and Diane still had to come to school."

She watched Leah bite the corner of her lip and then shrug her shoulder bones. With a big sigh, Leah scooted over close to the foggy window. Olympia scooted up next to her, squinting to see through the dripping rain on the window.

A white station wagon with sides that looked like wood lurched down Old Town Road. It rocked to a stop with a squeal of the brakes. Then it leaped forward with a grind of rubber. A big, red dog stood on top of the car. His frilly Irish setter ears flapped in the wind. He looked like a soggy dog-king, riding the bucking car into battle.

The lady driving the car was curved over the steering wheel, her mouth moving with angry, silent words. She kept looking up at the car roof and stomping on the brakes and then the gas. The red dog hunkered down, fighting the start-stop motion of the car.

The lady pushed on the gas. The car bucked forward. Then she stomped on the brakes. The car squealed to a stop again. Squeal. Push. Stomp. Squeal. Again and again and over and over, all the way down Old Town Road.

"Oh my," Miss Brinker said, not looking at the yowling busload of kids anymore.

Every time the car braked, the dog's nails

screeched across the metal roof: squeal-screech-squeal-thump-bang.

"Blarney's scared of storms. That's all."

"Really?" Olympia asked. "I've never heard of no dogs afraid of storms as bad as that dog."

"And thunder."

Light flashed overhead. Blarney crouched low, trying to hide himself.

"And lightning," Leah added.

"And lightning," Olympia agreed.

Blarney barked and snapped at nothing. Leah's mom reached the bus and pulled off to the side of the road. She rolled down her window and stuck her head out into the rain. She started yelling something up at the dog. Blarney shook rain out of his fur and then Leah's mom shook rain out of her hair, wiping her eyes.

"Stupid dog," Leah muttered, making Olympia laugh.

"Hey, what did that new girl say, O'limpet? You better tell us."

Ignoring them, Olympia sat back against the seat while Leah pulled a notebook and lunch box onto her lap.

"They don't need to know anything about nothing we say," Olympia said as she handed Leah her pink pencil box. "This is our seat now, on this bus. Don't forget that."

The bus door creaked open.

Olympia watched as Leah stood up and started to walk down the bus aisle; then she stopped, turned around, and gave Olympia a shy wave, ignoring all the other kids.

Leah's hair was the color of red honey and looked just like a silk ribbon cut right out of a sky full of the sunset. It was a red, honey ribbon made of silk and sunset, Olympia thought as she waved back.

7. Handprint

The whale's mouth squeaked open and the whale spit Leah out. She jumped into the rain. More lightning and another rattle of thunder drowned out the sound of laughing kids. On top of their station wagon, Blarney threw back his head and howled—a mop of soaked fur and misery.

The drippy, dark sky broke open like a bag of marbles. Fat raindrops exploded against the asphalt.

Leah ran through the rain, laughter skipping and dribbling out of the bus behind her.

Her little brother, Bobby, bumped into Leah's back, trying to beat her to the front seat of their car. He always tried to beat her to the front seat. He made sitting in the front seat of the car into some kind of race with a good kid prize at the end. Truthfully, it was the first time she remembered that she had a little brother all day, because there had been so many other things to worry about on the first day of class in a new school. She had worried about her skirt falling off or her lunch box being stupid or being behind in math. Her little brother wasn't even on the list. He tried to push around her, but he was too slow. She pushed back and won the race, throwing herself into the car.

Mom shrugged her shoulders. Her curly hair hung in moppy, wet strings on her cheeks. She explained through tight lips that she would try to tie Blarney up next time. Blarney thumped over Leah's head. She could hear his nails digging at the metal. His howling sounded lonely out there in the rain. Her brother whined in the backseat of the station wagon about having to sit in the back. It was his turn to sit in the front, he kept saying. Leah always got to sit in the front. He sounded bratty.

She glanced back at him. Rain dripped off the stiff bristles of his crew cut and ran down the upturned curve of his nose. He stuck his tongue out at her and crossed his eyes. He had green eyes too, but they were paler and smaller than hers, and usually hidden under the brim of a baseball cap. He kicked the back of her seat and then wiped his nose on the sleeve of his shirt. Then he started complaining about his new teacher, Miss Rhodes, because she smelled gross and had funny stiff hair.

As the bus pulled away, Leah pressed her face to the foggy window to see through the curtain of rain sheeting down. The back of the bus looked like a worm-wiggle of laughing children, but even through the rain and wiggling tangle of children, Leah could see the happy, frantic waving of one small, dark hand.

When Olympia, her new friend, pressed her palm to the bus window, Leah smiled. There would be a mark on the glass when the window dried—a handprint. Leah pressed her hand against the car window, thinking how Olympia's hand was exactly the same size as her own. Leah hoped Miss Brinker didn't clean that window, at least for a while.

"Don't smear fingerprints on that glass. That idiot dog is making enough of a mess out of my roof." When the car started to roll forward, Mom stomped on the brakes. The car skidded over the wet pavement.

Mom headed for home with Blarney's nails raking across the metal roof of the car every time he lost his balance.

8. Walking Home

No one waved goodbye when Olympia gathered up her spelling book and her pencil box as she waited for the school bus door to open. No one said, "See you tomorrow." No one asked about her dog or wanted to know why her mom didn't pick her up when it rained. Most of the time, the other kids on the bus pretended they didn't see her.

That was okay.

She looked at her handprint in the fog on the window and felt happy. I'm here. I'm here, and I'm not going away. And now I have someone to hold hands with every day.

At the top of the steps, she held tight to the slick metal pole, waiting for Miss Brinker to pull open the door. The rain thrummed outside.

"You hurry on. It's coming down pretty hard again. Why don't you have a sweater on, girl? And in this weather too." Disapproval made her words come out short and sharp.

Miss Brinker didn't really want an answer to

her question. Olympia could tell when grown-ups were asking questions they didn't really want answered. The bus driver pulled the handle and the door squeaked open before she'd finished talking.

"Yes Ma'am, Miss Brinker, I sure will hurry. Thank you, Ma'am."

She was extra careful to be polite and always use her best company manners when she rode the bus. Not everyone from her street was allowed to go to the cheerful brick building on Main Street. "Don't give them any kind of reasons to be sorry that they let you go there. That's the best way to be when you're around that kind." That's what her daddy always told her. Her granny stayed quiet about the matter. But it was easy to be as nice as she knew how to be. She loved riding the bus to the fancy school with the big windows. She loved the way it smelled and the way her teacher's voice banged against the big, tall ceilings in their fourth grade classroom. She wouldn't make them sorry that she was there. No ma'am.

Olympia skipped down the steps into the rain. It was coming down harder now. It was the kind of rain that came down so hard that it bounced up when it hit the ground. It was *down and up rain*. That's what Granny called it.

Muddy drops splashed her socks before she'd gone far enough to feel the cold that beaded in her hair and then trailed down her face. She pushed her spelling book under her wool skirt, trying to keep it dry.

On her left the orange grove filled up with the sound of drumming drops, each one hitting the leaves with a ping. Before the rain, the grove had been coated in a haze of dust— winter dull and drooping. Now it sparkled. The jeweled drops of water formed bracelets that ran down the mossy trunks and splashed into the puddles collecting in the dirt.

When Olympia had walked to the bus stop that morning, the orange grove had been another one of the dirty, tired places where her father mowed and cut and trimmed, season after season, to support their little family. Then the rain had come and made it into a glittering place where the oranges glowed green, waiting to ripen. The rain was like magic—a cold, clean mystery that begged Olympia to stop for a minute, to watch and listen.

Or would have if Olympia had known enough to wear a raincoat or a sweater. She should have known it was going to rain. Miss Brinker had thought she should have known enough to have a raincoat. The bus driver acted like she'd known about the unexpected shower and that everyone who was smart should have known such things. But who could guess about the weather all the time? Not even Granny Mac could predict the weather every time; could she?

It was true that Granny Mac knew a lot of things like that: when storms were on their way; how to figure how far away the lightning might be; the best time to plant okra; the best way to settle an upset stomach with mint. But even she got it wrong once in a while.

Finally the chill and damp won, and Olympia started to hurry and then to jog and then finally to run past the symphony of falling water in the trees next to her. The slap of her feet hitting the puddles became another kind of music.

By the time she reached the tiny front porch of her house, she was wet to her goosebumps and hoping for something hot and steamy in a cup. There was a mist of dew across the panes of glass in the front door. The fog on the windows in the door reminded her of the school bus windows. Behind the glass her grandmother's lace curtains hung in perfect starched calm. They were like the apron her granny always wore: stiff, ironed, clean, and sun dried, like Granny Mac.

On a whim, Olympia pressed her hand into the damp of the glass. Trickles of water ran from under her palm to the window frame while rain dripped from the end of her nose. She laughed when she thought about having to polish her handprint from the front door. Their house creaked and flaked paint, but fingerprints and dirt were not tolerated, not when soap and water were easy enough to come by and there was a granddaughter who needed to learn the value of working hard. Granny Mac didn't always get the weather right, but Olympia suspected she always got the work right.

Looking at her handprint in the window pane she thought about her new friend, Leah. Her hand would make the same size print, because they were the same. The same height. The same weight. The same bones. She could feel it, the memory of how perfectly their hands had fit together. The idea made a wonderful tickle bloom somewhere down in her chest under the buttons of her blouse. It made her quit breathing and then have to take a big gulp of air to fill up the emptiness. The feeling was like having Granny Mac waiting for her in the kitchen with a list of chores to do and mint tea steaming on the stove to warm her up.

She admired the handprint again as the edges started to drip and melt. That was okay; the fingerprints would be there tomorrow.

She pushed her way through the front door, dripping water across her granny's clean wood floor.

"I'm here. It's me. I'm home."

9. First Day

That was how Leah's first scary day in a new school ended and the first day of loving Olympia began.

10. *A Pretend Place*

When Leah's family moved to the country, the orange grove next to their new house was already old. It wasn't large, only five acres, but the tree limbs of the citrus trees were so thick and heavy it felt large—big, old trees in an endless wild forest. It stretched from their property line to the corner where Old Town Road and Spring Hill Road cut across each other. The old grove filled the corner where the two roads crisscrossed.

The trees were common citrus, which some

called "white" or "blond" oranges, with a few grapefruit trees and tangerine trees mixed in. No one had planted anything new or fancy in a very long time. The grove was full of good old-fashioned citrus for good old-fashioned Florida frozen concentrate—nothing exotic, nothing fancy, nothing modern or new.

The grove men who worked the orange grove mowed in the summer. They fertilized in the fall. They picked fruit around the New Year. Like everyone tied to the dirt and seasons for their living, they followed an endless cycle, watching for breaks in the patterns.

To Leah and her brother, the orange grove felt like dark mysteries and enchantment and the wild forests of fairy tales. The tree trunks of the largest trees were covered with years of soft, green moss and lichens, an exotic and alien growth that softened the rigid bark beneath.

Branches as thick as fence posts cast long shadows across the sugar sand ground; the trees stood like straight rows of soldiers at parade rest, guarding whatever secrets were hidden on the far side of the marching rows. It was a wall of green, an orderly fortress.

At first, the two children played along the edges of the orange grove. They were reluctant to go too far into the center of the trees. It was there that the sun could not shine. It was too dark. The leaves were too thick. The air stayed too still and quiet in the heart of the grove, so they played along the edges, close to the open sky, and built a fort in the shell of an abandoned car they found in a pile of *junk at the back corner of the grove next to their house, but they did not play in the darkest part of the grove.*

They were never brave enough to go into the heart of their magical forest or to see what was on the other side.

11. Eyes Like Chocolate

It was a crazy day full of smells, the day Leah and her dad went to buy the baby calf. The air inside the Dandelion Wine Dairy barn dragged at her lungs. The tang of grinding cows' cud competed with the spice of fresh cow pies. The whole mix beat around Leah's head like the wings of too many flies. It was a mad rush up her nose.

"Don't wrinkle up your nose that way." Leah's dad poked at her with the toe of his boot. "This barn smells great. It smells like roses," he said. His nose made a whistling sound when he inhaled.

Leah took a deep breath and coughed. The dairy barn didn't smell bad—it smelled like too much. Leah wanted to say that to her dad. I'm not used to it, that's all, she wanted to tell her dad, but she didn't.

"Why that's the smell of a real, working farm. Soon our place will smell just as sweet. That's part of why we moved—a farm for you kids like I had when I was a kid, that's how ours will be."

He laughed. She closed her eyes when his hand rested on the top of her head. She pressed up against the pressure of his hand. He took his hand off of her head. When he turned and walked away, she stumbled after him.

A row of grinding jaws lined the sawdust aisle of the barn as Leah shuffled by in her rubber boots. She watched the slap-flop of the cows' tails and their big heads as the cows tried to kill flies—first with their tails and then with their heads. Their tails slapped at flies. Their heads flopped. Slung sideways into their bodies, their licking tongues left snail trails of slobber across their backs and sides. The cows' udders swayed big and swollen under their bellies.

A dozen tails flopped against a dozen black and white sides, a dozen heads whipped sideways. Slap-flop. Slap-flop. The cows' big flat teeth never stopped chewing their food. Like the smells, it was too much. All the moving and chewing and fly swatting distracted Leah. She stopped to watch the cows.

A disgruntled bellow followed by the sharp crack of wood scared Leah and pushed her to catch up to her father. He stood at the opposite end of the barn, in the big square of light at the open barn door. It seemed like he'd forgotten all about her.

A dairyman, as round and swollen as any of his milk cows, stood next to her dad in front of the calf pens just outside the barn. Inside each pen was a brand new baby crying for its mother. All the baby calves could hear and smell their mothers, and it made them frantic. They bawled and wailed, knowing the cows were close. They pushed their noses between the wooden slats of their pens. They tried to suck on the toes of rubber boots or the edge of water pails, and they cried, while their mothers gave their milk away to the milking machines.

"Now, that bull calf's a beaut," the dairyman said, pointing.

Her father settled a booted toe on the lowest slat of the pen next to the dairyman. The calf rammed and butted at the toe of her father's boot, trying to suck the dirty leather.

"Yep."

"Almost killed his mother getting this one born, and she's my top milker. Fine big bull calf."

Her father leaned over the rail and scratched between the calf's ears. The calf danced backwards. He reached for her father's fingers with a curling, slurping tongue. The farmer gave them a little speech:

"Now you got to know bottle-fed calves don't

always make it. They can die of scours and a bunch of other sh . . . stuff, but the scours though, that's always the worst."

Her father dismissed the farmer.

"Sure, I know all about that. I had one like him when I was a boy. I told you, girl. How 'bout this one?" her father asked without looking over at her.

Leah bent her head to look through the slats of the pen into the face of the desperate newborn animal. She reached to stroke the calf's searching nose. He licked at her fingers. His tongue felt like asphalt, curling around her thumb. The calf dropped his head in excitement to butt at her fingers. Leah pulled her hand back.

"He wants you to be his mom," the dairyman laughed. "He'd butt his head into his mother's udders. It's how they get the milk to start working."

The calf lifted his head quizzically, searching for her. Warm, brown fur and a white, blazed face tempted her to touch him again. His brown eyes gleamed, moon-wet and glowing.

The baby cow's eyes followed her every time she moved. With a happy surprise, she saw that the calf had shining eyes like Olympia's, her new school friend. They were the same warm, melted chocolate color with no other colors mixed in— perfect—and he had the same black eyelashes with that perfect curl. She couldn't wait to show Olympia the baby calf.

In frustration and confusion, the bull calf wailed his greedy hunger at her.

Well?" the dairyman asked. He looked at Leah and then at his wristwatch.

It wouldn't matter what she thought; her dad would buy the calf. It was like the farm cows he remembered from before—from when he had been a boy and happy. Her dad mostly did what he wanted, and she always tried to want what he wanted too. She shrugged.

It's why he moved his family to the country, to the rustling fields full of quail nests and cricket songs on Old Town Road—away from the Space Coast where he worked. So they could see, smell, and touch a place like the one where he had grown up. That's what he had said.

Would he have cared how much she missed the gang of kids from Rose Marie Drive where they used to live? Or how much she missed the sandlot games full of noisy bickering and the sidewalks? He would not have understood about the sidewalks. She'd spent big chunks of time scribbling hopscotch games on the sidewalks with hunks of drywall chalk the boys stole from construction sites.

Oh well. It wouldn't matter what she said. In the beginning, she had missed Rose Marie Drive like the calf missed his mother.

It wasn't that she didn't like the smell of country smells or the idea of baby cows or playing in an enchanted orange grove. It was being so far away from the other things she'd known all her life: fluoride in the water and drywall chalk on the sidewalk. Standing in the driveway of their house and watching the rockets race into the sky. Being the same as all the other kids and not the new girl.

It was Olympia that made moving bearable, with her dependable handholding and whispered secrets and shining calf's eyes. Olympia kept the frantic sadness away when the kids in her new school pointed at Leah, calling her "New girl with the grossed-out dog," or when they barked: roof, roof—roofy—roof, roof or chanted: "Dork dog, dork dog, Leah's got a dork dog.

Leah walked along the pen, the calf bouncing next to her, its tail whipping madly. She heard her father tell the dairy farmer what he would pay. Then they talked back and forth, but she didn't listen to the grown-up talk. Instead, she listened to the calf crying at her to be his new mother.

The calf came home in the backseat of their station wagon to a brand new pen stuffed with tenderly fluffed hay. A bucket of water and a little feed trough that wouldn't be used for months waited in one corner. For now, Leah and her brother would feed the calf from a baby bottle the size of a water pitcher. It would be one of their chores.

The calf cried like a baby all the way home. He

was their baby.

The first day, Leah and her brother fought over who would feed him from the giant baby bottle, but Dad settled the argument and fed the calf himself. He showed them how to hold the bottle propped against the boards of the pen, with the huge nipple tipped down, dripping milk. He didn't go into the pen or bend down where the calf was. He let the calf reach up to bump its boney head into the bottle. The way he would bump his mother to make the milk start flowing. The calf smelled the dripping milk and found the rubber nipple—a good enough substitute.

The five-day-old calf guzzled his bottle so fast that a foam of milk bubbled out of his nose.

The calf sneezed milk onto Daddy's boot, making Leah laugh. From then on when Leah and Bobby came home from school the calf waited for them like a puppy—a crying, sucking, starving, ninety-pound puppy.

He was their baby. He was her baby.

12. Lion's Breath

Sometimes when Leah played she pretended that her family had moved from Rose Marie Drive to lion country, especially when she walked through the grass of their pasture, grass that was taller than her head and made her think of broom straws and hot African Savannas. This was lion country. The grass was so tall and thick Leah couldn't see her way through; she had to listen her way through.

Blarney yipped, somewhere near the back corner of the pasture where the dirt service road curved around the edge of the orange grove next to their property.

She pushed through the thick underbrush of the savannah, following a game trail left by raccoons or deer or zebras. Lions' eyes blinked at her from secret hiding places. Lions' bloody breath swirled around her from clumps of grass. There was the sound of lions coughing while they dreamed dusty dreams among the golden stalks, and Blarney barking, of course.

She needed Olympia on this safari, because her new friend should be right here next to her—facing lions and death. A branch of lantana slapped her in the face as she pushed through to the far side of the pasture.

There was so much pretending to do, Olympia would just have to spend the night—a sleepover like the other girls at school talked about. Leah stopped and smiled at the idea; it felt right as it rolled around in her head and then in her heart. The other girls at school talked about sleepovers all the time.

Tomorrow at school she would tell Olympia about the dreaming lions in the weeds next to the orange grove, next to their new house, and about the baby calf with Olympia's perfectly melting eyes and about sleeping over. Tomorrow they would talk and make plans.

Leah pushed forward through the clumps of weeds that towered over her, thinking how they smelled like dry sunshine.

"Bobby," Leah yelled. "Bobby, where are

you?"

The lions faded away. Leah followed the trail through the flattened weeds that had been made by the little animals at night, but her brother's tromping back and forth had flattened the weeds and grass even more. What had been a game trail was now a path. The path was torn up where Bobby had dragged something to the back of Mrs. Lockerbee's orange grove. Leah followed the wiggly groove in the dirt. She knew he was out here somewhere, skipping out of chores again.

"Bobby, it's your turn to feed the calf."

The bottle of milk for the calf was waiting on the kitchen counter, getting cold and separating into two layers, a thin watery yellow at the bottom and a thicker foamy sludge at the top. Mom got mad when they let the bottle sit for too long, but it was not Leah's turn and Mom got mad when she got stuck with feeding the baby calf his bottle.

Mom hated the barn, the dirt, and the dust, but mostly she hated the animals. Mom must be missing Rose Marie Drive too.

Somewhere beyond the path, near the orange grove, she heard the rattle of metal against metal. She headed toward the sound of banging and clanking and somewhere Blarney's barking.

"You'd better answer me before I tell Mom on you." Leah had never walked this far into the back of the orange grove.

"I'm here. Behind the really mossy tree."

"They all have moss, silly."

"No, not those. The most mossy tree."

She followed the wiggly groove.

Bobby's most mossy tree grew in the last row of the orange grove, all the way in the back. Everything here smelled like a bottle of perfume, because a few trees were still blooming, out of season. The orange blossoms made Leah dizzy with their sharp bite of spice and sugar mixed together. The weather had been warmer this year—Indian summer that had become Indian fall, and now flowers bloomed out of season in the still mild winter. "Sweater weather" her mom liked to call it.

The branches of the most mossy tree dipped almost to the ground around a fat trunk covered in grassy velvet that was the color of spring. The tree was a fort. Its trunk was a pillar in a magic castle, covered in hunter green moss and shadow. Its branches curved and dipped toward the ground. Pushing through the outermost branches into that hidden place, Leah sat in the low-hanging curve of a branch. The soft, green patchwork under her hand was like the silk of the calf's ear. She swung her feet back and forth through the dirt. Breathing was like filling her lungs up with orange blossom perfume. This was a magical tree in a fairy tale forest. The tree's branches hugged her in its arms. It felt safe to sit here. The way it felt when she crawled under a blanket draped over a card table; it was safe, secret, protected, and for a moment she forgot about Bobby and baby bottles for baby cows.

13. Car-Fort

Bobby exploded through the wall of green

leaves behind her.

He yelled, "Hi, Leah," right in her ear.

She fell sideways off the branch into the dirt. Her heart beat at her ribs, as if her heart would run away if it could.

Her brother's face was covered with smudges of dirt, and there was a big rip in his green and yellow striped shirt.

"You stupid! What are you doing out here all alone?" she asked, brushing her hands against her pants to knock off the worst of the dirt.

"I'm not by myself; Blarney is here too. Isn't this a great place for a fort? But you can't be here, because it's just for boys and for Blarney."

"Well that's stupid. I'm here, and I don't see any boys or dogs."

He threw himself at a tree limb, grabbing it with his hands and dangling like a piece of fruit or a bat.

"My friends are boys. You don't have friends."

"That's not true." She pulled herself out of the dirt and brushed at the hem of her purple stretch pants. "I have a new friend. She sits right in front of me at school because of the alphabet, and she is smart, smarter than you."

Besides dirt, Leah had fallen into a clump of beggar lice, and a trail of beggar lice seeds stuck to her sweater. She started to pick the sticky seeds off—one by one—but they stuck to her fingers, and each other, and made her sweater knot up. Still, it was a fun tree, a magic tree.

"It's a good spot, Bobby."

"This is nothing." He let go of the limb,

dropped to his feet, then backed away, disappearing through the wall of leaves.

She followed him. A jumble of junk and trash lay just beyond the edge of the tree line. There was a rusty rectangle of bedsprings, a pile of canning jars, a stack of rubber tires, and, best of all, the skeleton of a Volkswagen Beetle Bug car. It still had a steering wheel and a windshield. Bobby had been busy dragging bits of junk from here to there; she could see where he'd pulled hunks of two by fours and scraps of plywood through the sand.

"The tree is just a tree, but this is a fort," he said. "It's a car-fort for boys and Blarney, not girls."

Leah pushed past Bobby to look inside the empty wreck. He was so silly.

"Don't be gross and stupid."

He'd made an effort to push the leaves and rubble out of the inside of the car and fix up a floor of sorts. There was a hunk of old carpet that Mom and Dad had torn out of their new house that he'd thrown on the ground inside the car. That carpet must have been heavy to drag all the way out here across the pasture.

Leah was surprised at how much work he'd done all by himself, when he was always too little or too tired when it came to chores or any other kind of work at home. Leah poked around through the piles of junk.

"How about we sit in those tires for seats? I'll help you do it."

She could tell that he was torn between wanting her help and wanting to keep the car-fort all to himself. He kicked at a pile of empty tin cans with no labels. Then he scratched at a mosquito bite on the side of his neck. From under his baseball cap, he looked at her and nodded.

"Come on, we'll roll the dirt out of them." Leah headed to the pile of tires that was taller than she was. "Climb up and kick the tire on top off, and we can roll it around until the dirt and spiders come out."

He scrambled to the top of the stack like a monkey. A tangle of weeds stuck out through the center of the pile of bald, peeling rubber. He pushed the tire on top free. Leah jumped out of the way as it bounced and rolled.

She chased the tire until it slowed, wobbled, and then crashed onto its side.

"Help me! With two people it'll go fast."

They managed to stack eight tires inside the wrecked car; two for the driver, two for the passenger and four in the backseat. When they were confident that the spiders and grubs were all rolled out of the abandoned tires and they were stacked right, her brother plopped down in the tires behind the steering wheel. Leah sat in the tires in the passenger seat.

"Where shall we go?" Leah asked, trying to keep the fun going. Sooner or later they were going to fight, but not just yet, she hoped. Her side of the car still had a door. She leaned her arm out of the empty hole where a window used to be.

"Back to Titusville, where all the good friends are; where we belong." He wiggled the steering wheel back and forth. A trickle of dirt dribbled out of the steering column.

"There are fun kids here. Right? You can make new friends."

She said it exactly the way she'd heard Mom say it. It was no wonder Bobby rolled his eyes at her. What about the laughing, pointing, and joking of the kids on the school bus that first day of school? Had the kids in his class teased him the way they had teased her about their car-riding dog?

Her brother wiggled the cracked steering wheel back and forth harder.

"We had a fort in Titusville. The tree fort, remember? It even had a psychedelic trapdoor and a big purple mushroom."

"You don't even know what *psychedelic* means."

"Yes, I do. It means painting a big purple mushroom on stuff."

He started to turn stubborn.

"Well, it was a far-out trapdoor," he said.

"You mean the trapdoor that one of your friends opened behind you, and you fell out of backwards, and busted your head open?"

"It wasn't their fault; I missed the mattress on the ground with my head." He glared at her and then went back to pretending to drive.

"You would never have your own car-fort back there."

"I don't care. I liked our other house."

Leah knew he didn't mean he missed the row house on Rose Marie Drive that was exactly the same as all the other row houses on Rose Marie Drive. He meant that he missed the yards full of kids. He missed the sandlot stickball games and snitching drywall. He missed the games of red rover and dodge ball and writing his name on the sidewalk. What he meant was that he missed the neighborhood full of kids their age.

Leah could hear Blarney thrashing through the underbrush in the woods behind the orange grove. Past the woods there was a swamp and then a river. Would that dumb dog have enough sense not to run all the way to the river? Bobby didn't seem worried.

"Can't we make friends here too?" she wondered out loud.

"I don't want to."

"Well, I do. I already have a friend." *I do. I do have a friend.* It wasn't a guess or a question, not anymore. "Her name's Olympia." She waited for him to say something to her, to say that he was happy for her good luck, but he just pulled his shoulders up to his ears as if she was going to frog him in the arm.

"A girl. Just another stupid girl."

She leaned over and punched him in the arm. She was surprised when he didn't hit her back or threaten to throw a rotten orange at her. He must be really sad about moving if he didn't feel like fighting back. Leah tried again.

"Girls aren't stupid. It was my idea about the tires, and Olympia's not stupid. She's nice and she's smart and she has curly eyelashes and when she comes over to spend the night she'll love our car-fort."

"No girls, Leah. Girls are . . ." He was trying to think of a word bad enough, she could tell. Instead he said, "Girls are dumb as coons."

32

Bobby said it just the way he'd heard their dad say it. It didn't make sense when Daddy said it, but it really made no sense when Bobby said it. Raccoons were smart; they even washed their food. She'd seen it on *Wild Kingdom.*

"Olympia is too nice and smart."

"So what? I found this place behind the most mossy tree, not you."

"You'd better quit being mean about it, or I'll tell."

It was Leah's worst threat, next to socking her brother in the arm. He ignored her and tried to act like he didn't care, so he kept turning the steering wheel back and forth. He refused to look at her, and his lips got all pinched up and white.

That's what he did when he wanted to act tough and not cry, pinch up his lips like that. It just made him look mean and grumpy and stubborn. It made him look sick to his stomach.

"I am too going to tell mom on you. You're out here cutting the fool, Mr. Far-Out."

She would tattle on him if he didn't quit being stupid about girls. And there was something else, the reason she'd followed him out here. What was it she was supposed to remind him about? Oh, that's right—Mom had wanted him for something. She tried to think what it was, but the car-fort had taken all her attention and made her forget. Maybe it was something about cleaning his room?

She sighed, shivered a little bit, and thought about how warm it would be sitting in the barn cuddled up next to the calf. That is, if the calf didn't try to suck the buttons off her sweater, then her sweater would get soaked and she'd be cold again.

"Oh, I remember now. It's your turn to feed the calf and you're goofing around out here. You're in trouble, mister."

He ignored Leah and pouted.

The sun had started to slip way. All day the air had been cool but not cold, and as long as she stayed in the sunshine and kept her sweater on it was warm. However, as soon as the sun began to drop away, the air turned to ice.

She felt the cold air on her ankles first, because her favorite pair of stretchy pants had gotten too short in the last year. She had finally grown a little bit—not much, but some. She was still one of the smallest kids in her class—her and Olympia.

Now her pants pulled way above her socks whenever she sat down. When she sat in the passenger side of the car-fort, her legs flopped over the edge of the tires and her feet dangled—there was a lot of bare ankle hanging out. Her ankles looked like knobby bones covered with freckled chicken skin. They looked like skinny, white sticks.

She twisted her feet in circles, trying to warm the bare skin of her ankles. It wouldn't work. The sun would not stop sinking and the air would not stop getting colder. Her dusty white socks didn't come up high enough to keep her legs warm either. Sometime last year they had shrunk too, once in a while disappearing into her shoe and wadding up under her heel.

Bobby spit in the dirt, acting tough. He was such a brat. Why did he have to make being nice to him so hard? He made tattling on him about the car-fort easy. If he was bratty when Olympia came over she'd pound him. Forget about tattling.

Not *if* Olympia came over to spend the night, but *when*. Time to get brave and ask Mom. Who cared what Bobby thought?

She watched a black speck as it crawled up the side of her sock. The speck didn't budge when she brushed at it with the toe of her tennis shoe. She brushed harder, but it kept crawling. There was another crawling black spot, and another. Leaning forward she saw a dozen tiny, creepy dots on her socks and ankles. They had marching, twitchy legs—ticks. There were ticks marching up her legs, looking for bare skin to dig into and blood to suck.

Leah screamed and smacked at her socks.

"Ticks! On me, it's ticks!"

She pulled her pants' leg up above her knees. Ticks trailed up her leg, creeping higher and higher. She kicked wildly and then toppled out of her seat of tires and crashed into Bobby. He fell sideways out of the car.

"Hey, you knocked me over!"

"Ticks! I can't get them off."

Bobby crawled away from her. When she crawled after him she could see the tiny seed ticks on his ankles, on his socks, crawling all over his Keds tennis shoes.

"They're on you too! Run!"

He didn't bother looking. He ran. For all their bickering, if she panicked, he panicked. Even with all his big talk and stubbornness, he knew enough to run when Leah started hollering, even if he did think that she was just a dumb girl.

He took off and headed for home.

Leah passed him still screaming. Bobby yelled then, too, his voice higher and squeakier than Leah's. Thinking it all a great game, Blarney joined them on their wild, screeching retreat from the car-fort, barking every time they yelled as they ran all the way home.

14. Forever—Almost

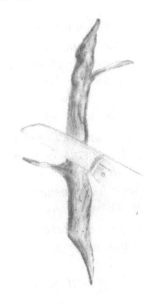

Orange trees can live a long time. With the right amount of sun, rain, and fertilizer, citrus tress can live a hundred years or more.

Through an ancient practice called grafting, citrus trees can live forever—almost.

Where a branch would grow there is a young, tender bump that is called a bud graft branch. A bud graft branch is a little piece of branch cut from the first tree. A horticulturist, a fancy word that means a tree maker, cuts the bump from an older orange tree or a tree that the gardener wants to keep alive so that it can continue to produce fruit. It will be exactly the same fruit as the original tree. It is the same wood, the same leaves, the same DNA as the original orange tree. It's like a piece of a puzzle.

Then a "T" shape is cut into the bark of a different tree, a poor, sour kind of tree that makes bad fruit, but that has strong roots. Its strength is in its roots. It's called sour stock or rootstock, and it's used for the trunk for the bud graft of the sweet fruit. A grafted tree is like two trees in one.

The cut in the bark of the sour stock or rootstock makes a little pocket—the other piece of the puzzle. The bud graft is pressed into the t-shaped cut and slid up under the bark of the rootstock tree. It's like pushing two pieces of a puzzle together. The gardener keeps the puzzle pieces low to the ground where the graft can get the most nutrients, water, and sap.

A graft is also like an open wound—if it's bandaged properly, it will heal. A graft is like a transplanted heart, like a transplanted heart that has to be taped together. When the sap flows like blood, the two trees heal, growing together forever—or almost forever. A grafted tree has roots that are wild and fruit that is sour, but the branches are whatever the gardener has grafted to it.

This is how orange trees can live almost as long as forever.

When Leah moved with her family to the fifteen acres on Old Town Road in the country, the orange grove next to them was already old.

15. A New Old School

It looked like a building that smelled old, the
way a cedar chest smelled old when it sat closed up
for too long.

Her old school had been brand new, and her
new school was old when she started going to it.
Evegan Elementary had been built in 1924 out of
red bricks and hopeful intentions. To be a real town
you needed a serious school, and Evegan wanted to

be a real town—the way Pinocchio wanted to be a real boy. The school was old now and Evegan was still not a town, just a place—a spot on Highway 46. It was a place to stop for gas between Fordsan and the coast. It was one red light and a gas station that sold milk. And even though rockets raced into the sky fifty miles to the east, Evegan was still a little place on the map, not even a town.

The front steps of the school were coated with one layer of white paint for every year the school had been standing. The steps stuck out on the front of the red brick rectangle building like an apron on a fat lady's tummy. White columns held up a front porch roof and looked like the hat over the fat lady's apron. Big, solemn windows watched for the buses to arrive. Panes of glass sparkled in the steamy morning light, outlined in white trim.

The ceilings inside were high. The wooden floors boomed. The one center hallway echoed. There were only four classrooms and an auditorium that divided the building neatly in two. It was a building full of the smell of chalk and damp and floor wax.

Leah's new old school was a building where smells came to stay and never left.

16. "Happy Hair"

It was like being lined up in a row of toy wooden blocks in Mrs. Ward's class. Leah and Olympia sat one behind the other in alphabetical order—*B* for Breck before *C* for Crooms, their desks touching. Every student at Evegan Elementary had their own desk. The back of Leah's seat bumped against the flat top of Olympia's desk. Their school desks were old-fashioned with all the pieces connecting: a flat wooden desktop with a slot for a pencil, attached to the desk's seat on the right side with a metal pole. The seat made a cube with an open, metal cubbyhole for books and papers. At her old school everyone sat at big shiny tables, but here the desks were like the school—used and scuffed, banged up on the edges, nicked but clean.

The desks of the kids with names that started with *A, B,* and *C* were pushed against the left side of the classroom, against the wall under the big windows. It was a nice spot when winter sunlight danced into the room through the heavy panes of glass. Dust motes glittered and streamed through the window in thick rays of sunshine.

Sitting behind Leah, Olympia pulled a black, plastic comb through Leah's hair. Static electricity crackled with every careful stroke. While the other kids hunched over their worksheets, pencils scratching across their papers, Olympia combed her friend's long, red hair. Leah's hair draped over the back of her seat in a curtain, almost touching the top of Olympia's desk. It felt impossible, too soft to be real.

"How you want your hair today?" Olympia whispered into Leah's ear. It made Olympia giggle when Leah shivered.

"You tickled my ear," Leah said, turning her head a little bit so that she could whisper back. "Can you make braids all over just like yours?"

"Oh sure, my Granny Mac showed me; except your hair is so slippy soft, like a baby's hair, it might be harder to do up than mine."

Leah shrugged her shoulders. She sounded a little disappointed when she said, "I wish my hair was like yours. It looks like it's going to a party all the time. It's all twisty like that chocolate and vanilla ice cream in a cone."

"My Granny Mac calls it my 'happy hair.'"

Olympia shook her head, making her barrettes dance at the end of her four pigtails. A pigtail bounced against her cheek. Why would Leah want any other kind of hair than her own? It was a little bit silly to want someone else's hair, especially when your own felt like a puppy's ear—or a pony's nose. That's what Leah's hair was like: velvet and puppies.

Leah's head sagged backwards with the drag of the comb and then again when Olympia pulled it through a rubber band into a ponytail. Leah loved to have her hair combed, and as long as Olympia wanted to play with her hair, Leah would sit with her hands folded on top of her desk, her eyes closed and a half-sleepy smile on her face. Olympia felt like that too when Leah unbraided and re-braided Olympia's pigtails. The feeling was like that curl of anticipation Olympia felt low in her stomach when she thought that Granny Mac might have warm brownies waiting for her after school. Olympia liked the system they had worked out, and tomorrow it would be Leah's turn to braid Olympia's hair. She had taught Leah how to comb her stiff black hair until it glowed.

The rubber band made a popping sound when it broke, making Mrs. Ward glance over at them.

Fixing each other's hair was as good as reading books or eating homemade rolls in the lunchroom or the hope of warm brownies.

Mrs. Ward stood up and searched the room for popping rubber band sounds and random daydreaming. Their teacher walked through the rows of desks, her panty hose full of scratchy cricket noises—scritch, scritch, scritch. There always seemed to be too much of Mrs. Ward for her clothes or her panty hose.

Olympia heard Leah smother a giggle with a cupped hand as Mrs. Ward chirped closer. The comb caught in her red hair as it bounced with Olympia's own silent laughing. The teacher focused a frown at them.

"Girls, are you two done with your work? Never mind. I know that you're done." She rustled to a stop, her voice tight. "Olympia, did you print your paper neatly?"

Of course her paper was printed neatly; it was a pointless question. Olympia always printed neatly and spelled correctly and had the right answers, just like Leah.

"Yes, Mrs. Ward." Olympia placed the comb carefully on her desk, her eyes dropping. She folded her fingers into a still, careful tent on the desktop. Maybe it was time to get the evidence out of sight. She tried to pull the comb under her hand with her pinky finger.

"Whose comb is that? Does it belong to you?" Mrs. Ward picked the comb up from the desk with two fingers. "Where did this come from?" She held the comb straight out, away from her body.

"It's my daddy's, Mrs. Ward. He loaned it to me to have this morning for my hair and to bring to school."

In front of Olympia, Leah sat still and quiet, half turned in her seat. She was like a marsh rabbit when it's afraid it's been spotted by a hawk. Leah kept her head down, and let her hair fall around the sides of her face like a curtain. Olympia kept her voice small as she explained about the comb.

"Haven't I asked you two to stop fooling around with each other's hair? And haven't I asked you two to stop this more than once?"

"Yes, Mrs. Ward," Olympia said. She hated being in trouble the same way she knew Leah hated being in trouble.

"Yes, Mrs. Ward." Leah's voice sounded small, and that made Olympia feel bad for her.

Olympia listened while Leah tried to explain.

"But we're all done with our work and our homework."

"I'm sure you are," Mrs. Ward sighed as she looked at the rest of the class. "I wish everyone else could be as quick about finishing as the two of you."

She snapped her fingers at one of the kids behind them and said, "Trevor Dalton, the answers to that worksheet are not outside the window or on Becky's paper. Eyes on your paper."

Mrs. Ward looked at the comb she held with two fingers; her mouth wrinkles bunched up.

The comb looked sad in her teacher's hand, its teeth missing. Why hadn't Olympia noticed that it was broken before now? It was funny how she hadn't noticed it before, those broken teeth.

"You two—stop fooling with each other's hair. This comb is dirty and greasy, and it's not appropriate when you're at school." She paused and looked at them. "Olympia, let your daddy keep his greasy, nas . . . his comb at home."

"Yes," they said together.

A hand shot up on the other side of the room.

Distracted, Mrs. Ward shook her head and said, "I'll keep this thing." She jiggled the comb at Olympia.

Another hand shot up as the first hand started to wave back and forth. Pulled to those needy hands, she finished with Leah and Olympia.

"You two go to the library and find something to read, and stop fooling around with each other's hair. I mean that."

She walked to her desk and dropped the comb into the top drawer next to all the other bits of junk she took away from her students. Olympia watched as Mrs. Ward wiped her fingers on a handkerchief carefully—one finger at a time.

Olympia wanted the comb back.

"But . . . that's my comb . . . my daddy let me have that comb."

"Go on," Mrs. Ward said, dismissing the whole thing.

Shocked that the teacher would take away something that belonged to her, Olympia said it again, but under her breath, "But it is my daddy's comb."

Mrs. Ward didn't seem to care.

17. Among the Books

In the end, getting extra time with the books in the library made up for feeling stupid about the comb, and getting to read and talk about books was almost as good as brushing hair and whispering secrets in each other's ear.

It wasn't a real library; it was just some books on bookshelves. Olympia, who had been allowed to go to Evegan Elementary, had watched as Mr. Tucker, the janitor, shuffled the books from here to there as the four-room school outgrew itself. He kept moving the library books all over the building. Mr. Tucker had moved the library twice, just since Leah had started going there.

When school started that year, the books had lined the one and only hallway in the school, but every kid who walked to the bathroom tended to stop and flip through a good picture book and forget about going to the bathroom. Then Mr. Tucker tried to convert a storage closet into a library, but there had been no place to keep his mops and buckets. Then, after Leah had come to school, the books went back into the hallway for a while. Now they went into the auditorium.

The pile of library books was in the auditorium all along the walls, tucked next to the lectern, lining the apron of the stage, and stacked on extra desks. The county school board kept threatening to send portables to help with the over-crowding problem at Evegan Elementary, but parents were horrified that their charming four-room schoolhouse would become a mess of temporary classrooms, so poor Mr. Tucker kept wandering around with his arms full of library books.

Leah and Olympia liked the books in the auditorium because there were squares of carpet to sit on and plenty of space to stretch out. They could flop onto their stomachs and read without worrying that some first grader needing to "go potty" might trip over them or a janitor's mop would crash down on their heads.

Unless there was a school assembly or they were having the annual spelling bee or everyone was getting a lecture about flushing paper towels down the toilets, the auditorium made an okay library.

Olympia liked it fine.

She and Leah were two smart, good girls, so people tended to forget about them when they were in the auditorium-library, and that made them both happy.

18. Bookends

Olympia loved the dog books. Leah loved the books about horses. They both loved a bunch of books called *Myths from Around the World.* Leah's favorite was a book about Polynesian myths and legends, and Olympia liked the stories from Ancient Greece, partly because of her name, which was like the name of Mount Olympus where all the Greek gods lived.

All the books they liked were chapter books: books full of words with a few pictures to stare at when they got tired of reading, and for when their eyes wore out and the words started to swim like fish all over the page.

Olympia watched Leah as she flipped through the pictures of beautiful, mixed-up Hawaiian islanders. Leah had told her that she thought the women beautiful with their brown skin and long black hair.

"Would you eat your son if you were the king, and it was the law?" Leah looked at the picture of the cruel cannibal king who almost ate his son by mistake. It was her favorite story.

"But I wouldn't be the king. I would be the queen," Olympia said. She flipped through one of the *Weekly Readers*, which was like a newspaper for kids.

"Okay, but would you do it? Eat a human being, a person—your very own kid?" Leah sat cross-legged on a purple square of carpet, her back to the rows and rows of wooden, folded auditorium seats.

Olympia thought for a moment.

"Would I know what I was doing?"

"No, 'cause your son is all wrapped up in leaves, trying to teach you a lesson about not eating people."

Olympia thought about this for a while.

"You always do that," Leah said.

"What do I do?"

"Think before you say stuff."

"Well, my Granny Mac says folks like folks who think before they start yapping. Don't you like it?"

"Sure. I like that you don't start talking as soon as I stop talking. Not like my brother who can't wait to start telling me why I'm stupid." Leah rolled her eyes. "Well, are you done? What have you thought up about the king of the cannibals?"

"Well," she said, dropping the *Weekly Reader* into her lap, "if I were queen of the cannibals, I'd have to say, 'No way, honey,' to the king, and then I'd cut the prince free. Then I'd make a speech—just like the Doctor Reverend King."

Leah knew that name. She'd heard that name on the six o'clock news when her family ate their TV dinners. It was one of the names her father always said something about. He never waited for the newsman to stop talking.

"What would you say in your speech?"

"I'd say that we're all made of the same stuff, and if you don't want to get eaten then you shouldn't eat nobody else."

Leah glanced at the face of the island prince peeking out from between palm fronds. The pictures in the book dripped color and purple shadows and were washed with soft highlights. His tribe was trying to cook him over a fire pit. The prince's father stood in the background looking grumpy about his dinner being late. Leah felt bad for the prince. It was probably hard to get cannibals to eat fried Spam or bologna.

Leah looked up and saw Olympia smiling her beautiful smile at her; it reminded Leah of the moon when the moon was big and round and full.

"And then I'd save the day."

"What if people liked eating other people so much that they wouldn't stop, even if you told them to stop because you're the queen?"

Olympia thought some more.

"Well, I'd say, 'Try these ham hocks my Granny Mac just cooked up.'"

Leah laughed and then stretched her legs out in front of her.

"Is that your favorite kind of food? Ham hocks?"

Ham hocks smelled like bacon boiling. Leah's dad cooked them sometimes in a big boiling pot of collard greens. Her mom called it "hillbilly food," and that made her dad mad because he was born in the mountains where the miners dig up the coal. He said *hillbillies* wasn't a very nice name for people who lived hard and worked hard and were hardly ever old when they died.

The bell rang for the end of school. Miss Rhodes, the newest teacher at the school, was the after school bus monitor, and would be on her way to hustle everyone to their buses. The clanging bell made Leah jump and Olympia sit straight up. They hadn't gotten to talk about their favorite colors or best birthdays or Leah's dumb bunny of a brother. There was never enough time at school for talking or hair brushing.

The question popped out of Leah like a soap bubble over a sink full of dinner dishes.

"Do you want to come over and spend the night at my house sometime?"

Olympia sat up even straighter and smiled. *If happy could be a color, it would be the color of the sparkle in Olympia's eyes right now*, Leah thought.

"When would that be?"

"I'll have to ask my mom. Then you can teach me to braid hair like your granny, and you can see my new baby calf. He has eyelashes like yours and big brown eyes. He jumps and chases us and wants to suck our elbows. His tongue is like sandpaper."

Standing up, Leah pushed the book of myths back into its tight, airless space on the bookshelf. She was thinking about Olympia spending the night. She thought she should warn her friend.

"Sometimes I have bad dreams, though. I dream that the calf gets sick and dies; I might wake you up when you spend the night if I have a bad dream."

"Oh my granny knows about baby animals. Don't you worry; you don't have to have bad dreams about that. She knows about doctoring up all kinds of things."

Olympia stood up and started to straighten the stack of *Weekly Readers*.

"So do I. I have bad dreams once in a while, too."

Olympia walked over and took Leah by the hand. They held hands and walked back to their classroom to get their homework.

"What about?" Leah finally asked. "What bad dreams do you have?"

"Oh, 'bout getting eaten by cannibals like a big ole ham hock."

Their giggles bounced off the walls like ping-pong balls.

19. Winter Burning

Granny Mac liked to tell Olympia that the seasons in Florida had a lazy way of coming and going. Fall was more often than not late, and sometimes showed up in the middle of other people's winters. It could be a neat trick to tell when autumn ended and winter began because the leaves and the temperatures were falling at the same time.

Olympia always knew when it should be winter—there was a special smell. It was time for winter when she walked home from the bus stop and the smell of Granny Mac burning leaves reminded her that frost was made of teeth. It smelled like frozen glass and gingerbread men that were burned on the edges. It smelled like the color brown.

Before she passed the mailbox in front of Preacher Bookman's church, she could taste the smoke from the burning leaves in the back of her throat. The smoke drifted up and down Spring Hill Road and snaked in and out of the open windows of the wooden houses that lined each side of the street.

She walked past Preacher Bookman's church. That's the only way she could think of the church her grandmother went to; that it belonged to Preacher Bookman, the way he always complained about roof leaks and rotten porch steps—like it all belonged to him, those porch steps and leaks. The church's clapboard siding, clean and white, was like a shout of hallelujah. The pointy roof didn't look like it needed fixing. It looked like a rocket ship pointing to heaven.

Every Sunday, Granny Mac was at church sitting in the third pew, ignoring the grouchy pastor so she could hear the angels singing, because angels hardly ever notice things like leaking roofs. That's what Granny always said. She made sure Olympia was sitting right there listening for angels too.

It was Granny Mac's way, the church going. It's the way her grandmother had grown up, working hard all week and church on Sunday. She wasn't one to have cookies waiting for Olympia when she got home from school, because it wasn't the way Granny Mac had grown up. Her school days had stopped at eighth grade, and cookies were for special days like the day you were born or the day your maw forgot where she belonged and didn't come home at all. On that day there were gingerbread cookies and oatmeal raisin cookies, and Granny Mac telling a body not to fret over things that could not be helped. Oatmeal raisin cookies tasted like the happiest and saddest days of her life.

Most days there were chores waiting to be done like raking leaves in the winter and washing windows in the spring. That was Granny Mac's way too—work before cookies.

Olympia walked home from the bus stop not expecting cookies, and she knew better than to ask if she should help out with whatever needed doing.

She followed the smell of burning leaves to the backyard where Granny Mac waited next to her burn barrel. Smoke poured from the rusty oil drum. Someone had hammered holes in the side of the barrel, making a half moon and star design. Light from the fire inside poured through the holes, and Olympia loved to stare at the moon and stars made of shifting, fluttering fire.

Granny Mac waited for Olympia. She leaned on a leaf rake, looking like she might be made of toothpicks tied together with strips of leather shoelaces. Her boney shoulders humped forward in a frozen shrug. She wore her frizzled white hair pulled back low on her neck, twisted into a hard, tight knot. Over her yard-chores dress she wore her work apron with the big, frayed pockets. The dress was homemade, a faded blue shirtwaist.

Olympia dropped her books on the tiny back porch behind the house and picked up the leaf rake that leaned against the porch railing. She walked to the edge of the backyard, where their yard ended and Miss Lockerbee's orange grove began.

The orange grove behind their house was one of the ones that her father worked and tended for the white folks. Those trees, row after row, meant groceries and rent money to her father and granny and, one day—maybe—college for Olympia. She listened to the rattling leaves of the orange trees for a moment and then started raking the dead leaves in their backyard into a manageable mound of leaves.

Granny Mac turned her watery eyes on Olympia.

So what did they learn you today, girl, up there at that fine school?"

"Hmmm . . ." Olympia considered the highlights of her day. "Spelling, I did pretty good, and the best part was when we talked about outer space and the stars." She tried to think of a way to bring up her friend Leah and getting to go to her house and sleep over sometime. She started making a new pile of leaves.

"What about them stars?"

"Oh, we learned just how far away everything is, especially the moon, because we're going there soon in a rocket."

Granny Mac made one of her *harrumph* noises, waiting for more information.

"Did you know that the moon is 235,000 miles away?"

"Is that far?"

"Well," Olympia said, loving the chance to talk about school, "If the earth was the size of a basketball and the moon was the size of a tennis ball, you'd have to stand way over there in Miss Jolene's patch of collard greens to get an idea of how far off things are in space. And we have to race the Russians to get to that old moon first."

Granny Mac walked over to Olympia's first pile of leaves and, using her rake like a big spoon, scooped up leaves for the fire. That was the thing about her granny. She looked about as strong as a stick bug, but she could still get out in the yard to rake, scoop, and burn leaves when other people were stuck in a rocking chair. The fire crackled and snapped, sparks flying up in a pretty, swirly rush. The wind shifted a little. The smoke drifted away over the grove.

"Well, it is the way of things to want to be winning. But it all seems a lot of trouble for not much. What do they think they're going to find up on the moon besides green cheese?" Granny laughed, coughing a little bit. "To my way of thinking, it seems a silly race to win."

"I like to win. So does my friend Leah."

Granny Mac shuffled over to scoop up more leaves.

"What friend's that? I ain't heard you say that

name before."

"Oh, she's just some new girl who rides on my bus and sits right in front of me at school." Olympia tried not to sound too excited. It wouldn't do to get "all riled up" as Granny Mac would say, because that would make her granny suspicious.

"Her family bought one of those baby cows from the dairy to take care of; you know, the ones you have to feed with a baby bottle. But she's afraid it might get a little bit sick. I told her you knew some good old medicines for sick cows."

Granny Mac sucked on her remaining teeth, nodding.

"Well, that I do, learned it from my granny, who got in trouble for knowing too much about such things from time to time. I'll think on it and tell ya something that you can write down for me, something to help your friend. You got to watch for scours or some I know might call it the squirts."

Olympia knew that Granny Mac liked to be consulted on matters of being sick and getting well. A new thought came to Olympia; something she'd never thought of before. Maybe, in a different world, Granny Mac might have wanted to be a nurse or even a doctor. She tried to imagine Granny Mac wearing a white doctor's coat instead of an apron with big pockets.

"Where these folks live?" Granny Mac asked.

"Just down the road, pretty close to here. She gets on the bus right before me."

Olympia didn't want to tell her grandmother where Leah lived. She couldn't explain why, but sometimes Granny Mac didn't like new ways of doing stuff too much. Better to wait for Leah to ask her mom about spending the night. Better to wait. Better not to have Granny Mac say no or worse have her ask her daddy and have him say no. It was much better to wait and give out new ideas a little bit at a time.

Olympia had gotten that idea from church. It's how Pastor Bookman said that God worked when he wasn't working in mysterious ways. Sometimes God doled out information here a little and there a little, so as not to get people all riled up before they were ready.

Olympia thought it a good way to go, especially with someone like her Granny Mac.

20. Dead

That night Leah Breck's heart stopped.

21. Dead or Dreaming

Leah could tell that her heart had stopped because she couldn't hear it any more. She could hear Blarney barking—somewhere far away, probably over the rainbow. Fire crackled and snapped and there was something like music over the rainbow where Blarney barked, but her heart sat like a stone in her chest. It was a hollow, silent stone. There might have been someone singing the Miss America song, but that's how bad dreams were sometimes, most times—silly and sad and disturbing all at the same time.

In the nightmare, her ears worked better than her eyes. Smoke filled her eyes. There was fire and smoke and singing. She could smell the smoke but not see it, because she was dead, of course.

Right before she had died in this crazy dream, she had been busy pounding at a sealed door, yelling, "Let me out! Let me out!" But they couldn't. Once they closed the space capsule there was no way out; the door was stuck shut.

"Death trap. Death trap. Dork-dog riding on a roof."

This was one of the bad dreams.

She woke up and gulped air like a fish drowning on dry land. Her heart started up again and smashed against her rib bones. Bits and pieces of the dream flip-flopped in her head.

She needed a glass of water and to catch her breath and to try to hear her heart beating. She got out of bed and stood in the middle of her bedroom. Her bare toes were chilly, almost cold. Holding her breath she listened for her heart, and realized that no one can hear their own heart beating, except in dreams.

The cold floor sent winter chill up into her feet, breaking into shivers under her skin as she walked to the kitchen.

Ever since Daddy had come home from work early the day of the terrible rocket ship fire, worried about his job, sad about the fire and the three dead astronauts trapped and burned, Leah had been dreaming the fire dreams.

Leah and her brother knew about the accident. No one told them about it; they'd overheard Mr. Cronkite on the six o'clock news saying the names of Grissom, White, and Chaffee in his most serious reporter voice. They'd listened without listening to the world of parents and their troubles and worries. It was more like absorbing information the way a sponge sucks up water than being told or taught. While Leah and Bobby were busy doing the growing up stuff, they absorbed bits and pieces from the puzzling world around them, and three dead astronauts was another one of those grown-up puzzles. Then another piece of the puzzle happened when Daddy started coming home from work long after Leah and Bobby were in their beds, filled up to the top with sleep and dreams.

22. Hearts and Doilies

"They never had a chance." Her dad was talking, his voice coming low and hard from the kitchen. He was talking about the fire again.

The sound of his voice was like a beacon, and Leah shuffled toward it. She could hear her mother asking a question. When her mom and dad talked that was her mom's job, to ask questions in the right places and then be quiet.

"The door might as well have been welded shut. The door opened inward; they couldn't force it open. It just couldn't be opened from the inside because of the pressure. It was over in three minutes."

"Isn't that just horrible?"

"Techs on the outside could hear them screaming, but couldn't do anything fast enough. Every department is under the gun, you know," he paused. Leah imagined him raising his glass to drink. "Lots of late nights—overtime at least—trying to finish the investigation, probably a trip to Houston."

"Well, that's something, isn't it? The overtime, I mean." Glass clinked against the kitchen table.

"Congress is screaming. The press is howling. Everybody wants to blame someone."

She stumbled from her bad dream into theirs.

"Leah, you're up; what is it?" Her mother swept the bottle with the words that were somebody's name into the little cabinet over the oven. Leah thought of it as the amazing appearing and disappearing bottle. It made her think of a magician's rabbit—now you see it, now you don't.

"I had a bad dream," she said, and walked to the sink. A glass appeared near her hand. She turned on the faucet.

"What was your dream about?"

Leah shrugged.

"Can't remember."

Leah tipped her head back and swallowed and looked at her dad through the bubbly bottom of the glass. The thick glass made him look squat and froggy. It made him look tired, and her mom patted Leah's head without looking at her, keeping her eyes on her husband. She swiped her mouth across her flannel nightgown sleeve.

She turned to go back to bed and then remembered.

"Mom? I need Valentine's Day cards for my class soon."

Standing at the sink, Leah's mom swished hot water around inside the water glass.

"Sure. Remind me when I go to Zayre's."

"One for every person. A really nice one for Mrs. Ward."

"Okay."

"And I want to make a nice one for Olympia, she's my best friend," Leah added. She didn't want one of those dumb packs of cartoon valentines with Bugs Bunny eating a carrot. "Maybe one with lace on it, like a paper doily and some glitter too."

"Is she a nice girl?" her mom wanted to know. "Does she ride your bus?"

"Go to bed." Her father's voice was like the

period at the end of a sentence—done, finished, stop.

"She's my friend. Can she come over and spend the night?"

"That should be fine," her mom said and hustled her out of the kitchen.

"Bed!" And that was the end of another sentence.

She wanted to give her tired, sad father a hug or maybe get a kiss goodnight, but his breath would make her have to hold her breath, and then he would stare at her like he was looking through the bottom of a water glass if she tried to kiss him.

She gave her father a little smile. He didn't smile back.

It was embarrassing. Why couldn't she be better at making him smile at her? It was a great puzzle.

"Goodnight," Leah said.

No answer. She went back to bed and dreamed of dancing lace hearts until morning.

At dinner the next evening, Daddy announced that he would have to go away to Houston, and that Leah would be in charge of taking care of the baby calf. Her stomach felt like she'd just gotten up from a bad dream, because baby cows died—all the time. What if the calf got sick? What if she didn't know what to do? What if Mom didn't know what to do?

Bottle-fed baby cows died. She'd heard the grown-ups say it. Her stomach heaved and she could taste acid in her throat like when she got sick and threw up, because she was the oldest and she would be in charge of something that might die.

Being the boss tasted like throw up.

The little calf had become a funny, sweet friend, chasing Leah and her brother around the pen. Once he was full of milk and not trying to suck their fingers off, he got curious and playful, full of bouncing steps and leaps. He liked to explore his pen. He liked to sniff the corners of the metal barn that made two sides of his pen, where the spiders spun their webs. He liked to sniff at Leah's hair. He liked to bounce into the air with the sheer joy of having friends like Leah and Bobby. The calf was happy at their farm and always would be. Believing that was easy.

After dinner, when Leah was in the shower and she knew that no one could hear her, she cried until she gagged, because the taste of acid on her tongue had not gone away after supper. How could Daddy leave? He knew the right way to hold a newborn calf's bottle. He knew about farm stuff.

Leah cried because she didn't know how to take care of something that might die.

Before Daddy left on his trip, her mom and dad fought.

"We agreed."

Dishes crashed in the sink as her mother complained. Leah worked on the little bit of homework she had in front of the television. The whole house smelled like dinner; fish sticks and ketchup. She could hear them all the way on the other end of the house.

"No, *you* agreed. Like you always agree with yourself. You had to have the *Green Acres* life, complete with baby animals sucking on bottles. What's next?"

"Janet, I'll bring a godda . . ." his voice trailed off as a drawer slammed somewhere in the kitchen and utensils rattled, "gorilla on this place if I want to. A month. That's what it will be."

Leah sat absolutely still even though she knew they couldn't see her all the way up in the living room. It was a habit. It was always better not to be noticed when their voices stabbed at each other like that. Sometimes before Daddy left on his trips he would tell her little brother to be the "man of the house," but sometimes he didn't even say goodbye. They would wake up, and he'd be gone like a magician's rabbit or that bottle in the cabinet over the oven.

"Have Carlton or Butch Westly come over if you run into any problems. Westly's got two hundred acres of cattle; he's down the road."

"That little man who spits tobacco on my shoes? I can hardly understand him when he talks. I'm not even sure if he's speaking English, he's so country."

"What do you want me to do? What else do you need?" Their voices got sharper. The crashing dish noises got louder.

Stay. Don't go. She wants you to stay. That's all. Stay and be someone who knows about baby animals and living in a place without sidewalks. It felt good to tear the sheet of notebook paper under her hand free. She crushed it into a crumpled ball, and then threw it against the wall.

23. Boss of the House

Mom needed Dad to be home the way Leah needed Dad to be home. They all needed that. She wanted to tell him that before he went away, but instead she slipped out the front door to escape the sound of their voices and the sound of dishes landing hard against the stainless steel sink.

Without streetlights, everything disappeared at night: the grass, the pond, the orange grove, the fences, even the curve of the earth. In the dark, Leah stumbled down the front porch stairs, because there was no way to tell how far away the steps might be. Walking around in the dark was like being dizzy. She didn't want to turn on the front porch light. She didn't want Mom and Dad to know she was outside in the dark.

Instead of seeing she had to listen, which was kind of funny, she thought, because she'd come outside so she wouldn't have to hear. A light, crisp breeze teased the ends of the palm fronds by the front door. They made a dry, rattling sound. A branch scratched at one of the windows. Leah sat down on the bottom of the steps and waited for Blarney to find her in the dark.

She heard him snuffling the ground before she saw him and then he sneezed right in front of her. Leah reached out and waited for the goofy dog to come into her arms. He sat on her feet and then licked her face.

"Blarney dog, I shouldn't let you lick me." She stroked his head and ears. "You almost messed up my whole life forever, riding on top of our car." He panted hot breath in her face. "Blarney, you are a stupid, stupid dog. And Bobby is stupid too. How can he be the man of anything? That'd be like making you the boss of something."

Her eyes adjusted to the dark, but she could only see the barest outline of the dog's head. He looked like he might be smiling at her.

"Mom will try to be the man of the house, but she'll just cry about it and not know what to do because of her allergies—to dust and hay and baby cows and probably all the dark that's out here."

Blarney scratched his ear with his hind leg and then somewhere beyond the big river and Titusville there was a rumble and a boom that sounded like thunder or a rocket shooting off from the Cape. Blarney lifted his head, and the boom sound came again. The dog collapsed against Leah's legs. He whimpered and squatted. The side of Leah's pant leg felt strangely warm and then wet and then cold.

Ammonia burned her nose.

"You peed on me!" With both hands she shoved the shaking dog away. "I hate you. I hate what a 'fraidy cat you are. I hate you."

She kicked out at him but missed. He disappeared into the dark, whining and growling. Leah's hands smelled like ammonia from touching her wet pants. Horrified, she wiped her hands on her T-shirt.

"Stupid idiot dog," she hissed at the invisible animal then stood up and yelled into the darkness, "I'm afraid I won't know what to do, but at least I won't pee on anybody!" Leah's stomach lurched again, this time from the smell of ammonia and worry.

She stood on the bottom step of the front porch and went over and over it in her head: how to mix the milk, how to hold the bottle, how often to drag the bottle out to the barn, how to clean the pen. Mom would help her, she would, and Leah would work hard to remember everything and get it right, the way Dad had shown her. Then when he got back, he would be proud of how responsible she had been and smile when he saw her.

Out in the dark, thunder boomed.

24. School

Leah was glad for school. It was nice to get to go to school—sometimes—where there were grown-ups to tell you what to do all the time and no one expected kids to know much of anything, even after they taught you stuff.

25. Boy Trouble

Olympia and Leah sat next to each other on the cement steps tucked behind the auditorium. The steps didn't lead anywhere anymore. The back door to the auditorium had been blocked up. The classroom walls jutted out on both sides of the auditorium, just far enough to form an alcove that felt hidden and secret from the gangs of kids that hooted and hollered all around them on the playground. It was chilly in the shadow of the building, so they sat in the sun, side by side, their knees pressed together.

A boy from their class named Wayne stood in front of them, flipping an uneven fringe of hair out of his eyes, and trying to be funny. He glared at Rhonda Miles, a lonely girl who was in the grade above them, but who liked to drift over to Olympia and Leah at recess.

Wayne snorted and rolled his eyes at everything Rhonda said.

"What do you mean, 'You're going to town'? Fordsan's not town; it's just plain old Fordsan."

Rhonda shrugged her boney shoulders and brushed at a fly that was trying to explore the corner of her eye. She was one of those girls that seemed to be made of too many bones that were held together with rusty wire and too much hair. Her eyes bulged behind her glasses. She turned to Leah and Olympia, ignoring Wayne.

"My Auntie Reba is taking me tomorrow. I don't have to come to any school tomorrow," she said.

Rhonda dropped her hands to her hips and twisted her thin body so that her yellow plaid skirt whipped back and forth around her knees. The fly landed on the black frame of her glasses. She swiped at it, accidentally knocking her glasses half off.

"That's the dumbest thing I've ever heard of. We go to Fordsan all the time to buy feed; it's no big thing to go there." He kicked at the dirt with his boot.

Olympia dismissed Wayne with a wave.

"Sounds really fun, Rhonda."

"I've never been to any town as big as that Fordsan town," Rhonda confided. "I'm going to go shopping and eat at Dairy Queen and visit the Piggly Wiggly." The wind tugged at the hem of her skirt and tangled her hair. She pulled her sweater together and buttoned the top two buttons.

Olympia saw Leah smile.

"I've never been to Fordsan either," Leah said.

"Yeah, but you lived in a real-sized town," Wayne countered. He scuffed his toe through the dirt again as a dirt devil grew out of the ground at his feet, showering dust across the steps where the girls sat. Everyone squinted. Wayne suddenly changed the subject.

"Hey, L-E-A-H, how's Stormy, that dumb dork of a dog?" He sang Leah's name like a song for jumping rope.

The girls brushed sand from their ankles and shoes.

"That's not his name. His name's Blarney, not Stormy."

Olympia dismissed Wayne and pointed him away, while Leah frowned. He inched closer. Rhonda hovered, listening.

"Go away, Wayne. We're talking."

Reaching over next to her head, Olympia snapped a Hibiscus branch free, one fat, shiny leaf quivering at the end. She waved it through the air over their heads. Wayne tried to snatch it away.

Olympia laughed at the way Leah tried to frown him down.

"Wayne, go away and leave us be."

Olympia waved her flower wand over Rhonda's head.

"Rhonda, I pronounce you queen of Fordsan Town. Go there and have a shiny, good day. I command it."

Rhonda giggled. Wayne lunged harder at the branch, knocking into Leah's side. She pushed him away.

"Why can't you leave us alone?"

Wayne shoved his hands into his pockets. His eyes crumpled up above the hard line of his mouth.

"Why are you friends with these dumb girls?" he said. He ignored Olympia and kept looking at Leah. "You're just a new girl here. Ain't your dad an astronaut or something groovy like that?"

Olympia watched Leah shake her head, her hair flipping back and forth like a silky wave.

"He's helping the astronauts get to the moon before those Russians get there."

"They won't beat the Russians if your dad burns up any more of those astronauts."

Shocked, Olympia listened as her friend fought back.

"No one burned them up. It was an accident, and my dad is building an escape hatch now."

"Too late." Wayne stuck his tongue out, kicked dirt at Rhonda, and grabbed at Olympia's branch.

"You stupid boy. Stop being so mean," Olympia said. "Besides, I'm going to be one of them astronauts someday." She could feel her hair bouncing.

"You can't. You won't."

Olympia glanced over at Leah, whose face was

white all over except for two fiery splotches on her cheeks.

"Mrs. Ward says that girls can be doctors and not just nurses if we want. Why not be astronauts too?"

Wayne spit in the dirt at his feet and kicked at the glob.

"My dad says that girls can't be astronauts 'cuz they're weak."

Olympia couldn't think of what to say to that and had to take a deep breath.

"Well, your dad's just wrong."

When Wayne looked at Olympia, his eyes got small and mean.

"No, he's not wrong," he said and stabbed a stubby finger at Olympia, "because you're a girl and nothing but a dumb darky."

Someone gasped; it took a minute for Olympia to realize that it had been Leah.

"That doesn't even make any sense . . . you . . . you . . . gross dork. Sticks and stones can break my bones, but words can never hurt Olympia or me or Rhonda."

Backing away from Wayne as if he had started throwing acid, Rhonda abandoned Leah and Olympia to the argument and the name-calling and ran off to the playground. She glanced back over her shoulder at them as if she expected to see someone's head spin around. Olympia couldn't blame her.

Wayne stood with his arms stiff at his sides, his hands balled up into fists. He looked like a lump of mean that had frozen solid.

Leah tensed next to her. Olympia could feel her friend trembling.

Olympia didn't know that she'd started crying until a tear trailed down her cheek and dripped onto the front of her corduroy jumper; it shocked and embarrassed Olympia to have Leah hear Wayne call her such an ugly name. She could feel Leah looking at her, but then Leah grabbed her hand and squeezed.

Jumping to her feet and still holding Olympia's hand, she leaned forward and shoved Wayne backwards with her free hand. Caught by surprise, he stumbled backwards, his mouth hanging open like a startled puppet.

"You go away, Wayne Conley, and shut your mouth unless you want to catch flies or my fist. You made Olympia cry, and I won't let you do that, and I don't like you."

"Girls are so weird," he said.

He turned to leave, hesitated, and then reached over to punch Leah in the arm—hard.

26. The Winner

Leah rubbed her arm. Olympia leaned over and kissed the place where Wayne had punched her. Patting her on the back, Leah tried to comfort her friend.

"Wayne is a silly boy, and he's grosser than my dog and my dog peed on my leg the other night."

Olympia looked at her with eyes full of puffy tears and giggled. Tears skipped down the curve of her soft, brown cheek.

"But do you think I can be an astronaut?"

"And a doctor. You're the smartest girl in our class. Of course you can, and my dad will help you when he gets home from his trip to Texas. Dumb boy."

One tear still trembled on the edge of Olympia's lip as she smiled.

"Let's not think about boys." Olympia sat up straighter. "Let's play something, astronaut or Miss America? I'll go first." She jumped to her feet and climbed to the top of the stairs turning slowly, her hand on one hip.

Leah laughed when Olympia, in a funny announcer voice, pretended to ask herself, "What would you like to be when you are all grown up, Miss Florida?"

Then Olympia changed her voice to sound like a grown-up lady.

"Why I'm going to be Miss America and then an astronaut and then a doctor and then a mommy."

Leah watched Olympia as she spun on her toes one last time, and then walked slowly down the steps, her knees appearing and disappearing under the hem of her green corduroy jumper.

Leah sang.

"Here she comes, Miss America."

Olympia paraded to the bottom of the stairs and then bowed and waved.

"Not yet, I have to ask you a question. What would you like to do if you become Miss America?"

She placed her hand carefully back on her hip.

"I would like to be the first colored girl to go into space, and I would like to spend the night at Leah's house."

"Good answer. You're the winner."

27. *Tamed*

In February, when the oranges in Miss Lockerbee's grove were still green and hard but were starting to get round and fat, the grove boss came to disk the orange grove. Dragging the rolling blades of the disk down the rows between the trees, the tractor kicked up clouds of dust. The winter

wind caught the clouds of dirt in its teeth; spitting it over the trees, the pastures, and the black asphalt of the crossroads where Old Town Road and Spring Hill Road crisscrossed.

Some of the dirt from the orange grove found its way into Leah and Bobby's house. It settled on the countertops and floors. It sifted down through cracks and fell into the wrinkles of the bedspreads.

The grove boss made one and then two and then three passes, and then it was hard to keep count of the number of times he churned up the head-high weeds that grew between the orange trees back into the dirt. The rows between the trees grew smooth and even—beaten down by the man on the machine. He managed to transform it from a wild, magic place into an even, measured, controlled creation of the man on the tractor—a tamed space.

Leah and Bobby watched the man, wondering if he would find the car-fort at the edge of the orange grove and knock it down. They had to keep Blarney chained up so he wouldn't chase after the man on the tractor. The children watched and waited. Bobby paced. For him, slipping away to the car-fort was the only thing that made living in this lonely place worthwhile. He still talked about Rose Marie Drive like it was home and where they lived now as a very bad trip.

The baby calf and the other animals their father dragged home had started out fun in the beginning, but soon they became all about chores and work. The orange grove wasn't like freedom. It was freedom. The kind of freedom you couldn't pretend. Leah worried, but not like her brother.

It took two days to disk the orange grove smooth, getting it ready for when the grove pickers came with their tall ladders and stacks of wooden crates. For as long as the disk kicked up dirt and chewed down the weeds between the long rows of orange trees, the orange grove lost its mystery and bled magic the way it bled dirt into the winter wind.

28. Fine and Not Fine

The phone clicked back into its cradle. It had

been a short phone call. Nobody had talked to Dad except Mom.

"Your father says that all bottle-fed calves get the runs; it's nothing. We just need to get something called scours medicine. That's what he called it: scours."

She glanced at the list in her hand.

"I have to go and get a twenty-five-pound bag of scours medicine." Then half to herself, she said, "I wonder what that's going to cost."

She frowned when she saw Leah's face.

"Oh, don't look at me like that. We'll get it. We'll get the medicine, silly. There's a feed store in Fordsan. I'm sure it will be fine."
But it wasn't fine.

The more the calf drank, the worse the diarrhea got—even with the scours medicine. Leah and her brother were worried the first time that the calf refused to drink from his bottle. Usually he sucked so hard he collapsed the sides of the heavy plastic milk bottle.

After that, it was only two days before the calf started laying down more than it stood up. They tried to feed him while he was laying down, but the milk would run out of his mouth when he shook his head at them; it flew away in a spring-white spray.

It was a Saturday night when the children sneaked out to sit with the sick calf. The round moon climbed full bright into the sky, its light slashing through the paddock railings to shine in thick, white bars across the hay. The moonlight set fire to the straw with a clean, white glow, and its absence turned the corners of the pen into darkened pits. Spiders worked on their lacy webs in the corners of the stall. Mice chittered in their secret places in the barn rafters and behind the walls.

You can read a newspaper by a moon this bright.

Leah had heard her father say that about the brightest kind of moon—a full moon like this one. It seemed a silly thing to think of trying to do.

The baby calf lay in one darkened corner. Leah and Bobby had to be careful where they sat, because the hay was wet and filthy in spots from diarrhea.

Her brother held the calf's head on his lap.

"He just stays still now."

"Should we give him a name? You know he's not an it; he's a boy. "

Leah stroked the calf's ears. The calf lifted his head and sneezed. Snot spewed across the hay, and the moon's light made the drops sparkle. His nose dripped a little.

"Maybe we should call him Sneezy, like the Seven Dwarfs?" Bobby suggested.

"Do you have a cold, baby?" Leah ignored her brother. The calf tried to lift his head at the sound of her voice.

Her brother liked the idea of finding a name for the calf. They'd tried calling him a lot of easy names, but nothing had seemed right yet.

"I think we should name him Brownie or Spotty."

"No, those are silly. He doesn't even have spots."

A lonely mosquito drifted around the calf's ear, buzzing out of season, because it hadn't gotten cold enough yet to kill the bugs. The calf twitched his ear when the mosquito buzzed by and then dropped his head back into Bobby's lap. The moon shifted across the sky, creeping into the corner where they sat. The light made the calf's eye look like a tiny star or like a tiny bit of the moon had fallen out of the sky into the dark corner of the pen.

Leah thought how small the moon looked, even when it hung full in the night sky. She thought of how badly the astronauts who had burned up inside the rocket had wanted to fly all the way to the moon. They had wanted to be like Apollo and fly a chariot across the sky.

"We should call him Apollo. It's a big, strong name," she said.

"Apollo is a rocket, not a baby cow." Bobby sounded firm. "I want to name him Brownie."

"Not like the rockets. We should name him Apollo like that god from Greece, because Apollo the god didn't die."

"No. We should name him Brownie the Brown Cow."

"Too boring and not cow. Bull. He's going to be a bull."

"No it's not."

"Not what?"

"Boring," he pouted. "Okay, then let's call him Tank. Nothing's bigger than a tank, or stronger."

Leah watched her brother get all pinched up, his shoulders around his ears, his mouth an upside-down curve. It was like he wanted to fight about something, anything, and it made her want to hurt him for never listening to her or agreeing with her or even hearing her.

"Tank's a stupid name. I hate it."

"It's the best name ever thought up for a cow."

"He's not a cow, you stupid . . . Why won't you listen for once? He's a boy, a bull."

"He'll be big as a tank. You'll see, won't you?" He bent down and started whispering baby talk into the calf's ear, "Big, big, big as a tank. Tank, stank, lank, rank, kankity-kank-kank, yankity-yank . . ."

It was silliness. He was silliness. She had to make him understand for once.

"Tank is the worst name. Tanks explode. Tanks crash and burn and everyone inside dies, all burned up." The calf never flinched, even when she screamed. When Bobby scooted back away from her, she realized she was so angry she was crying big, hot tears that didn't drip but covered her face. Bobby let the calf's head flop onto the ground. "Tanks are ugly and mean and full of . . ." She couldn't think of anything bad enough to put inside of a tank, and that was more frustrating than Bobby. Bending down, she picked up a clod of filthy hay and threw it into his face. "That's what tanks are full of, and so are you."

She stumbled away from her brother's shocked face and the too still calf at his feet, ignoring the moon that traveled across the sky and sent a tiny piece of itself across the calf's fever-bright eye.

29. Chalk Dust and Kool-Aid

Olympia listened. Leah talked.

Leah talked about asking her mom about spending the night; she talked about her dad leaving and her annoying little brother; she talked and talked. Olympia liked to listen when Leah talked. With no brothers to bug her, it was pretty quiet at Olympia's house most of the time.

They stood outside on the sidewalk so they could bang erasers together for Mrs. Ward and chalk the dust out of them. Chalk dust puffed up around them like a dry fog. It was a reward to be standing outside in that fog of chalk—a prize for the smartest kids, the best school citizens.

Olympia made sure she banged the erasers as hard as she could while she listened to Leah talk.

"Our house was white with black trim, but my mom painted the front door red. No one else had a red door, but everyone had the same carport. Our grass was the greenest and all the kids came to our yard to play ball and Red Rover and Mother May I."

Olympia had always lived on Spring Hill Road at the edge of Miss Lockerbee's orange grove. She thought about her wooden frame house that didn't touch the ground but sat on stacks of cement blocks. Listening to Leah talk about Rose Marie Drive was like hearing about people walking on the moon.

Olympia banged away and listened.

"My mom was a Kool-Aid mom."

"What kind of mom is that?" Olympia asked. She watched chalk falling from the sky onto Leah's hair. It looked like fairy dust.

"That's when all the kids go home with a red mustache from drinking Kool-Aid."

"I don't have no mom to make red mustaches."

"Why not?"

"She went away when I was a little girl and left me with Granny Mac and my dad. I don't remember her at all. Granny Mac says my momma's not worth one minute's worry." Olympia would have told Leah about the lonely times when she thought she wanted a mom, but she didn't have words to explain how her chest ached in the middle of the night.

"What else did you do at that place you moved from?"

Leah tested her eraser against the side of the building where it left a faint chalk outline. She went back to knocking them together while she talked.

"In the summer the mosquito trucks would come around spraying smoke to kill all the skeeters."

"What for?"

"To spray fog that killed the skeeters. Me and my brother would run behind the truck in the smoke. It was fun. All the kids did it. My mom made us stop when the TV talked about DDT and poison and some other stuff."

Olympia shook her head at the idea of a mom stopping something so exciting and fun as running behind a fog truck. Is that what moms did? Maybe it was good not to have a mom. Granny Mac wouldn't care about such stuff.

"My granny thinks smoke is a good way to chase the skeeters off." Olympia tested her eraser against the red bricks of the school building. She couldn't see any chalk dust left over on the building.

"When you come over, we can drink Kool-Aid and play with Apollo. That's the name I want for the calf."

"Apollo, like from those Greek stories. It's good, that name."

Leah frowned, making worry lines between her eyes. Olympia knew that Granny Mac would tell her to stop scrunching up her face or it would freeze that way.

"He's got a cold and he poops a lot—too much." She sighed. "All the time; he has something called scours."

"My granny would know what to do to make him better. She knows all about fixing up stuff for cows and pigs."

"Maybe my mom should call your granny?"

"Can't. She won't talk on the phone. She's afraid that lightning will find her through the wire and burn her eyebrows off. She says her eyebrows are about all that she's got left that ain't moth eaten. Granny Mac's pretty partial to her eyebrows."

The lines between Leah's eyes disappeared. Instead, her mouth turned up, ending in her dimples as she laughed.

"You can tell me more stuff that your granny says when you come over."

Olympia loved the way Leah talked about the two of them spending the night—as if it was as certain as having a birthday coming up or going to church on Sunday.

"Okay, when?"

"My mom hasn't said when. She has to think about it."

Olympia thought she understood about mothers; Even Granny Mac had to think things over once in a while and she was just a grandmother and not somebody's mother.

30. *Bitter and Sweet*

Orange trees are not hearty. They're prone to root rot and disease and pests and freezing temperatures. They freeze when the weather gets too cold or stays cold for too long. Winter freezes can be hard on citrus groves and the men who take care of them.

When an orange tree freezes, the part that has been grafted on will die, leaving only rootstock. The rootstock is wild and the fruit that grows on rootstock will be sour and bitter. When a citrus tree freezes and the graft dies, the tree is said to have "gone wild." *It will become what it really is—a sour orange tree or a lemon tree with bitter fruit.*

The good, sweet fruit will disappear. The tree still grows. It will still have leaves and flowers and fruit, but the leaves will be tiny and stunted, and the fruit as sour as acid.

It will be that other tree, the first one, the wild tree grown and used for grafts for the sweet, better fruit. It's not wild like a bear or a lion. Actually, the tree has just gone back to being what it's always been—a tree that won't be able to make sweet oranges anymore, because a bad tree can't make good fruit.

The old churchgoers liked to point at the thorny, ruined trees in the orange groves after a hard freeze and say things like, "Bad can't come from good." "It's in the Bible," *they liked to say. It's a law that good fruit can't come from a bad tree. That's what the old churchgoers liked to say.*

31. Battle Cry

"Incoming!"

Leah automatically ducked. Her brother was a good shot. A fat orange exploded in the dirt next to Leah, and the war was on. She raced deeper into the grove, dodging around trees and through branches, getting as far from her brother's battle cry as she could get. The trees gathered her in. She stood still in their leafy reach and listened.

Her brother raced around, Blarney thrashing behind him. Leah lobbed a dangerous orange bomb over the treetops. The best orange bombs were rotten, but not too rotten; too rotten and they fell apart in the air; too fresh and they wouldn't blow up properly. Too fresh and they might give the little dork a knot on the head.

Leah raced for a hulking, old citrus tree five rows in from the edge of the grove, whose branches forked so low to the ground that it was easy to climb up into its canopy of leaves. The trunk was soft with moss, and its thick, shiny leaves overlapped and crisscrossed. It was like a watchtower, secure under the winter sky.

Leah climbed up the tree, gooshy oranges rolled up in her shirt, her heart thumping. Her little brother crashed into view, sweaty and breathless, loaded down with ammunition. As soon as she saw him, she pounded him with oranges. Direct hits. It felt good to watch him grovel around on the ground.

He was in the dirt, yelping and rolling.

"You blinded me!"

Juice and rotten pulp dripped down his face.

The memory of a soldier's broken face from the six o'clock news flashed in her head, and the number that was the number for dead soldier men so far away. Mom called it the "body count." *Counting bodies must be a hard job*, Leah thought, and then wondered about hand grenades, and booby traps, and if in a place with a funny name like Viet Nam anyone got to fight for fun with rotten oranges.

"I give," her brother howled. Blarney licked orange juice from his face. Leah pretended to have more oranges than she really did.

"You swear you give?"

He lay face down in the dirt and played possum. Blarney sniffed him and jumped back, the way he would sniff at a hognose snake when it curled up and played dead. Bobby didn't move. Just like a hognose snake—faking, she thought. The snake and her brother were both big, gross fakers.

She relaxed just as he twisted off the ground and came up throwing—a slushy orange that exploded against the tree trunk next to her head. While he raged at missing her, she laughed, lost her balance, and fell out of the tree. The dirt under the tree was still soft from being disked. It felt like falling into a sandbox.

"You can't climb up in a damn tree." Bobby stomped in a circle. Blarney tipped his head at him and wagged his tail.

"Don't say bad words," she said, but her nag was as automatic as his bad word. Her brother had been cussing since he could talk. He liked shocking Leah by trying out the new cuss words he had learned.

She laughed some more. He stomped to the trunk of the tree and looked up to check out her hiding place.

"It's against the rules."

"There are no rules when you're in a war with somebody. You just have to win."

The fight drained out of him like a flower wilting. He picked up a stick and smacked it against the tree trunk, but it broke into three rotten pieces. If there was one thing you could say about her little brother, it was that he played hard and mean, but he ran out of steam pretty quickly, especially if the other guy's oranges were juicer. He stomped over to where Leah lay in the dirt and, glaring down at her, shrugged.

Leah wanted him to admit he'd been surprised.

"That was a pretty good ambush. Don't you think?"

"It was okay," he said. "But I knew you were up there the whole time."

"No, you didn't. Blarney didn't even know."

Blarney whined once at the sound of his name, and then flopped down in the cool dirt near the big tree.

"I knew you were there."

She could feel the argument coming—on and on and back and forth, "Yes, I do," and "No, you don't." She was glad she had cheated a little bit and smashed him in the face; maybe she was still mad about the other night. Maybe. Leah tried to change the direction that the argument was headed.

"You don't know everything, you know."

He started up again.

She stopped him with something she knew he wouldn't know.

"You don't know when Olympia's coming to stay."

It was all she could think of to say to shut him up. She could tell he was impressed in spite of himself.

"Who says?"

"Mom does. That's who."

"Oh yeah, what day is that?" He was fishing, picking.

"Soon," she said. It was the only answer she

had.

"Sure. Soon."

Blarney got bored and padded off to flush quail. The soft, whirring flutter of birds' wings rose through the tarp of leaves over their heads. The sound of Blarney's barking bounced around the orange grove like a ping-pong ball.

"Yeah soon. But you can't follow us around." Better to make the rules now and not waste time fighting with him when Olympia came over. She could tell that it made him mad.

"I bet Dad doesn't know about your friend coming over. He wouldn't like it."

"Why not?" she asked, surprised.

Maybe Bobby knew something that Leah didn't know. A worm wiggle of worry came alive in her stomach. It was hard to tell about Dad; what he liked or didn't. He got mad all the time like Bobby. They were alike in that way. Sometimes it was hard to know what made either one of them mad— sometimes.

"Because she lives down that road—Spring Hill Road. That's why."

A car horn blared in the distance. *Honk. Honk-honk . . .*

Blarney jumped up and raced off, barking. Leah started brushing off her pants. It was time for supper. Mom honked the car horn when she wanted to call them home to eat.

Leah tried to think what there was about Spring Hill Road to get mad about or not like. There was a broken-down school bus next to the frail, white Spring Hill Road Missionary Baptist church. Most of the yards were small and had no grass, but they were all raked smooth and neat. Orange groves on both sides of the road pushed out between the tiny wooden homes. The row of houses on both sides of the road ended where the big ranch pastures began.

"What's down there that Dad wouldn't like?"

"All them people who live there," he snapped, waggling his head at her. "Those Spring Hill Road people. I heard Daddy say it."

Leah didn't try to understand her brother. It probably wasn't even true; it seemed so silly. Bobby was jealous. He was mean. He was a dumb boy.

"What did he say? About what?"

"Jig-a-toos. Spring Hill Road is where all the jig-a-toos live."

"Jig-a-toos! What's that? That doesn't even mean anything. You made that word up."

His arguing face started up—his nose wrinkled up, his mouth curved down, and his eyebrows crashed together.

"Jig-a-toos like my teacher and I hate her. She makes me take off my ball cap and color inside the lines. And she wants everything fancy."

Leah was tired of arguing with him about everything. She wanted to tell him that she loved Olympia. That it was easier to love Olympia than to love her own freckled, silly self that got red blotches when she cried.

She opened her mouth to explain about the loving and why his silly lies and stupid pretend words could not change anything.

The car horn honked again.

Bobby stuck his tongue out at Leah, picked up one of the rotten oranges at his feet, and threw it in her face. Then he took off after Blarney. Leah stomped, screamed, and tried to wipe her burning eyes on the sleeve of her turtleneck. Juice dribbled down her face and into her mouth. It was sour and full of acid.

Leah ran after her brother, who ran after Blarney. The juice and pulp on her face was sticky. Her eyes burned. She squinted and watched as Blarney wriggled underneath the barbed-wire fence between the orange grove and their pasture. He left a wad of red fur hanging on one of the barbs. That wad of hair looked like a trail marker left for an explorer—a clue.

Her brother threw himself between the strands of barbs after the dog and got his shirt hooked on one of the barbed wires. He didn't wait for Leah to help him get free. He hollered and tried to wriggle free by himself.

It was hard to wiggle through the barbed-wire fence by yourself and not get hooked. It helped a lot when two people took turns stepping on the bottom strand of wire to push it down with their foot. Then they pulled the higher strand up, as high as they could with their hand, making an open hole in the fence. It was hard not to get scratched without help.

Leah yelled at Bobby to wait and that she would help him get unhooked, and for him to stay and wait for her, so that he could help her crawl through the strands of barbed wire.

"Bobby wait! Help me!"

He ignored her and pushed through the strands

of wire.

Leah heard his shirt rip, and then he took off running. Her brother ran faster when he heard Leah yell. He was probably worried that she'd sock him once she crawled through the fence. She pushed the bottom wire down, and tried to duck low enough under the wire above her.

When she caught a loop of her hair in a twisted barb, she yelled, "I'll tell you who's a jig-a-too! You are!" A sharp prong scratched her shoulder through her shirt. She yelled harder, "And I hope it's a bad, bad word. I hope it's the worst word in the universe!"

32. Winter

Winter came during the night with a bitter rain and a wind that moaned and cried.

33. A Fine Kind of Music

"'This is our seat on the bus now.' Remember when I said that the first day you came to school?"

Leah smiled and nodded.

Olympia remembered saying it that first day when everyone had laughed at Leah because of her dog. For weeks after that when the boys had barked every time they saw Leah or Olympia, having a place of their own had made all the difference.

"Roof. Roof. Roof." The other kids had made the word sound like a dog barking.

It had been the best joke ever—for a while, but Olympia reminded Leah every day that something else would happen to make them forget. It always did. And it did.

On her way to the cafeteria, Pauline fell down the stairs and broke both her arms. It was all the other kids talked about from then on.

Olympia knew they would. She knew the kids at Evegan Elementary. She knew this place. She knew the trees that grew on the side of the road that they passed on the bus ride home from school, and she knew and loved the way Leah wanted to hear everything Olympia knew about.

At one sharp curve in the road, where the bus always groaned and leaned and the smaller kids slid across the hard plastic seats, she pointed at a scarred, old oak tree. Its branches dripped with Spanish moss that danced as the bus went by.

"That's sure enough a killing tree."

Leah gasped.

"Oh sure, because lots of people have been killed right there," Olympia said, pointing.

Leah's green eyes went round. Olympia loved when they did that.

"Killed in car crashes coming around that bad curve in the road. They smash right into that old tree every time."

"Wow, I've never seen a tree like that before." Leah slid over to the window so she could press her face against the window. Olympia slid closer and pointed again.

"You can see those marks on the road from cars slipping and sliding right into that tree."

Leah pressed her nose against the window.

"My Granny Mac says that's a good enough spot for haunts and spooks."

Olympia flopped back into the seat.

"Did you know that old Miss Henry has a donkey that likes to eat cigarettes?" Olympia said.

Leah stayed pressed to the window.

"I'd love to see a donkey like that," Leah said. "That would be amazing."

When Leah was excited her eyes didn't just get big, they turned shiny. Olympia loved that Leah's eyes were the color of moss and leaves and new grass.

"I know. Maybe someday you can come to my house, and we'll walk over to Miss Henry's and see that donkey that eats cigarettes."

They laughed at the same time. Olympia thought that when they laughed together it sounded like a fine kind of music.

Miss Brinker frowned at them in her long rectangle of mirror.

They shushed each other, and slid down below the top of the bus seat so they couldn't see Miss Brinker looking at them. They giggled.

In the seat behind them, Joanie Rayne started singing under her breath. The song spilled over the top of their seat like the cawing of a crow.

"Leah and Olympia sitting in a tree, k-i-s-s-i-n-g. First comes love, then comes marriage, then comes two girls with a baby carriage."

Leah started to sit up, her cheeks flushed pink under her freckles.

Olympia hissed, "Forget her. She's just mad

she doesn't know anyone who knows about a donkey like Old Miss Henry's."

Leah relaxed back down into the seat and slumped until her head was the same level as Olympia's.

"No, she's mad because she doesn't have someone like you to ride home with on the bus."

Smiling, Olympia felt as if she could sit next to Leah forever, telling her stories and watching her look amazed.

It gave her a feeling in her stomach like butter melting on toast. It was the same feeling she got when she held her cat Calypso on her lap or listened to Granny Mac humming while she quilted. The feeling was like a cat purring inside her tummy.

The bus ride home never lasted long enough to tell all the stories Olympia wanted to tell, or to watch Leah's green eyes get big and round like an owl's.

One day, when the bus bounced by one of Miss Lockerbee's other orange groves, Olympia pointed to the workmen carrying ladders. The wooden ladders were so tall it took three big men to carry them. The men stacked orange crates at the end of the rows—getting ready.

"Those are all my uncles, some are my cousins, and my daddy. They pick the oranges 'round here and work the groves. My daddy is the head worker. He's the boss man of the workers."

Olympia knew most of the men who worked for her father by name because most were family. After a long day in the groves, they'd come to her little house, eat Granny's chicken and dumplings, and get warm. They would laugh and talk and sing. She didn't tell Leah about what they said after the singing, when they talked about the honky white men that the Reverend King was fighting up over in Alabama. She didn't tell her about "black power," which was a whole new way of thinking about the old stuff. Olympia didn't know why she didn't tell Leah those stories, but she didn't.

In front of the orange grove, the bus hissed to a stop to drop off the Denton boys.

Olympia started to point at the men carrying ladders.

"That's Jesse Banks, he's my cousin; and that's D. B. Jones, he's from up north around Richmond, Virginia. They all come over to my house to eat and sing when they're done working."

"They don't look like they sing. They look dirty and cold."

Olympia looked at the men, their hands wrapped in rags and their coats ripped in spots and patched in others. One or two of the younger men wore their hair in great puffy Afros. It was a new style, and she wasn't sure if she liked it yet. Her cousin Jessie liked to keep a black hair pick stuck in his Afro right over his ear. Most of the men who worked for her daddy wore knit caps that covered their whole head right down to their ears.

"Oh, it's a dirty job picking oranges for white folks. That's what Granny Mac says about it."

"I wouldn't like that job."

"Not me, neither. That's why I'm a reader and a writer."

Leah looked at Olympia with her owl eyes full

of questions.

"My daddy, he can't read too good. He says that I need to read so that I don't have to climb ladders going up to nowhere over and over again."

The bus door squeaked closed.

34. Dog Jail

Blarney was arrested after a winter storm made up of angry clouds full of lightning blew through the area. It frightened the floppy-eared dog so badly that he tried to outrun it. The storm rolled and roared in from the East Coast, tearing through Brevard County, ripping down trees and knocking out power. By the time the storm blasted its way through Seminole County, Blarney was berserk. He took off and made it all the way to the bridge on Highway 46, halfway to Fordsan, before someone called the dogcatcher.

Mom had to drive all the way in to Fordsan to bail him out of dog jail. When Daddy called that night, Mom had done a lot of yelling and a little bit of crying.

Leah was afraid the kids at school would find out, and they would remember about Blarney and the car "roof." They'd pretty much forgotten all about the time when she was the new girl and had to be driven home in a car with a barking, red dog on top.

Leah felt lucky when no one found out about their dog being arrested.

There had been a lot to distract the other kids at

school; there had been Pauline's two broken arms, the rock-man had come from the Central Florida Museum to show them all kinds of rocks: rocks that bounced and rocks that burned and geodes that looked like mud on the outside but were dazzling magic on the inside when you busted them open with a hammer. The rock-man came all the way to Evegan Elementary to get them excited about coming to the museum in Orlando. Then the firemen from the new Evegan Volunteer Fire Department came to talk about fire drills and what to do if the Russians dropped bombs on all the fathers who worked at Cape Canaveral.

35. Valentine

On a Friday, Olympia and Leah sat on the school's front porch steps side by side, their legs pressed together. The steps were still winter cold from the night before, even in the late afternoon. The cement made their bottoms cold while the sun made their knees warm. The mercurochrome blooming under their matching white Band-Aids looked like red wildflowers.

Olympia held Leah's homemade valentine. It was ragged on the construction paper edges and creased in the middle from being touched and folded. Gold glitter covered the tips of her fingers and left a trail when she touched the scallops of the doily.

When Bobby had tried to snatch the tired valentine out of Olympia's hand, Leah had shooed him away. Nearby, a first grader sent a haze of chalk dust into the air. It swirled and drifted like a tiny cloud.

Leah watched Bobby's teacher, Miss Rhodes, as she talked to their mother, the sound of the teacher's voice rising and falling in a gentle wave. Miss Rhodes helped everyone get on the right bus. It was easy to like Miss Rhodes. It was her first year of being a teacher, and she was as new and exotic to Evegan Elementary as a new satellite spinning around the earth. She taught Bobby's class, and Leah had heard that she was from some big city up north, had just started teaching, and was excited and young and full of ideas.

Her skin was the color of dark caramel and her clothes were as modern and stylish as Jackie Kennedy's had been: wool suits with short jackets and big buttons. Her shoes and purse always matched. Her hair always gleamed. It was easy to like Miss Rhodes.

Mom had come to take her to the dentist and seemed pleased to be talking to the chic, new teacher from way up north. Miss Brinker was late. Her bus had broken down, and everyone was still waiting for the replacement bus. Kids waited in front of the school, twitchy and tired.

Miss Rhodes had walked straight over to talk to Leah's mom about something, probably Bobby and his bad attitude. Bobby hid himself behind the kid with the erasers when he saw who was talking to his teacher. Leah could tell by the way she had headed straight to her mom that whatever she wanted to say was serious. Miss Rhodes had a way of walking and talking that was so strong and steady. When she spoke she sounded like she had practiced all her speeches in front of a mirror, just in case.

Confident, cool, and smart—that was the way Miss Rhodes seemed when she wasn't in her second grade classroom. She'd probably never had boney knees covered in Band Aids and splashes of red medicine a day in her life. Someday, Leah would like to be able to talk like Miss Rhodes and wear Jackie Kennedy jackets.

"You might wish to speak to Leah, Mrs. Breck, about being more careful."

Caught by the sound of her name, Leah looked over up at the adults. She could hear surprise in her mother's voice.

"Careful? Is something wrong with Leah?"

"Did I hear that you and your family moved here recently?"

Miss Rhodes cleared her throat, folded her hands in front of her, and waited patiently for an answer to her question. She looked like she was practicing her best teacher's posture on her mom. Leah nudged Olympia with her elbow, who looked up and snickered at Miss Rhodes trying hard to be fancy and serious. She was the new teacher who always yelled at her second graders to be quiet and sit down, but they hardly ever did.

"We did. We bought the Gatlin house out on Old Town Road."

Their talk trailed off and was in danger of becoming all grown-up and boring again. Leah bent her head to the valentine in Olympia's lap, wanting to let their voices drift away.

"And Leah started school in Titusville? I've heard good things about the new programs in the Space Coast schools," Miss Rhodes said.

"They were trying something called *team teaching* at Oak Park Elementary, all brand new, like the new math program and pod classrooms." Her mother didn't sound all that convinced. "Leah's father works at the Cape. I thought the drive out here would be too much, but he doesn't seem to mind," she hesitated and then added, "and besides he's out of town a lot."

Miss Rhodes leaned closer to Leah's mother, and her words turned soft. Leah took Olympia's hand and squeezed it; they went still and quiet to be able to hear.

"You know, of course, that Leah is one of the few students here at Evegan Elementary that has ever been to a school any bigger than this one."

"There were over a thousand students at Oak Park her first year. I'm actually glad of the smaller school here. Now you were saying about Leah . . ."

Miss Rhodes looked past the girls on the steps to the squat brick building behind them. She waved at the building as if she was shooing a fly.

"I don't like saying so, but this is a much more backward school system," she hesitated, "than I . . . expected." She sighed. "Anyway, when I came here from Michigan to teach, I was hoping for . . ." She shrugged, shaking off whatever she was going to say.

"Well, never mind that; I'm so glad we've been able to have this chat. About Leah then, actually, I was asked to mention to you that we've had some incidences of lice and nits this year among the children. I've been talking to several of the parents. The faculty is trying to get the word out." Miss Rhodes reached up and smoothed her perfectly curled flip. Her black hair was glossy, straight, and styled. "Some of these children's people are as good as sharecroppers and still send these children to school with grease in their hair. We sent several children home last week with lice."

Leah remembered Rhonda crying in the hallway, standing next to a little blond boy that Leah had not known, waiting for someone to pick them up from school. Rhonda had been too miserable to look Leah in the eye.

"Lice? I don't know what you mean. I feel pretty stupid, but I've never . . . ."

"Actually, I never had either until Miss Polly, our school secretary, explained things to me. Some people call them 'cooties.' Little insects that live in the children's hair and lay their eggs."

"I had no idea." Leah's mother sounded as if she'd swallowed a sharp rock.

"Insects that live in dirty, greasy hair and lay eggs that stick to the individual strands of hair and are extremely difficult to remove. Miss Polly found some nits, that's the lice eggs, in her own hair." Miss Rhodes was using her best teacher's voice now. "I've been told that certain of the children bring them to school and give them to the other children. The children who don't . . .," she lowered her voice almost to a hiss, "well, who aren't as clean as they might be: possibly the negro children, and even some of the poorer white children."

"There are children here who've never been to a town big enough to have a beauty parlor." Miss Rhodes dipped her head toward the two girls on the school steps. "My mother owns her own beauty shop and made sure that my sister and I were getting our hair done professionally before we were out of elementary school. Good grooming was very important to my family. I don't remember my mother ever mentioning cooties." She dropped her hand, brushing the crisp pleats of her red wool skirt flat over her hip.

Leah watched her mother's quick look stab at Olympia, who had become a hunched lump next to her. Olympia squeezed Leah's hand so hard it ached. Olympia's other hand had tightened into a fist. She must have forgotten about the valentine in her hand; she'd crushed it into a wad of glitter and glue.

"Mrs. Ward, Leah's teacher, is a friend of mine and mentioned to me at lunch that Leah and her friend won't stop fooling around with each other's hair, sometimes using combs and brushes that have been brought from home. Mrs. Breck, I've been told that getting rid of lice is a real misery, especially in long hair like your Leah's. Some of the children here live in very poor situations."

Leah couldn't hear her mother's response, because their voices had faded away when they turned their backs to the two girls.

Olympia's voice was a whisper in Leah's ear.

"I don't have those things, those cooties."

"I know. I don't even care what those things are."

"Cootie bugs. Miss Rhodes is saying I have bugs crawling and living in my hair and at my house."

"Miss Rhodes didn't mean you." Leah felt icky. "She couldn't mean you."

"It's because I'm one of the poor kids, you know. She said it: sharecroppers."

Without looking, Olympia pulled her hand out of Leah's and started trying to flatten the wrinkles out of the crushed paper doily on the valentine. Leah put her hand over Olympia's, the valentine a ruined mess under their fingers.

"But Miss Rhodes has hair just like yours."

"No," Olympia said, shaking her head. "No, Miss Rhodes doesn't want hair like mine, like she had when she was a little girl. She wants white folk's hair. That's what Granny Mac says. 'Cuz some colored folks like her don't know who they want to be any more.'"

Leah looked at the neat part in her friend's black braids, and loved the way Olympia's barrettes danced when she dropped her head. She saw only the complicated, clever patterns in her friend's clean black hair.

Leah saw only Olympia.

36. Comb

Olympia watched Miss Rhodes pull a black comb from the pocket of her jacket and show it to Leah's mother. Olympia remembered a comb just like it going into Mrs. Ward's desk drawer—her daddy's comb. She remembered a comb with missing teeth that looked sad and useless, not like this comb with all its teeth.

The grown-ups moved too far away for the girls to be able to overhear.

Olympia pulled her books together when the school bus finally rumbled to a stop in front of them. She jumped to her feet and turned to say goodbye.

"You asked your momma to let me spend the night?" Olympia scuffed her toe against the bottom step.

"I said I would," Leah reassured her, smiling. "And I did and she says she's still thinking."

Olympia watched the smile fade.

"Miss Rhodes didn't mean you. You believe me, don't you?"

Olympia wanted to believe Leah. She wanted to forget how that black comb looked in Miss

Rhode's hand. She wanted to forget the names that boys like Wayne called her and the looks that made her feel lonely in a classroom full of white kids.

She turned to walk away and heard Leah calling after her.

"My bedroom is all yellow with big sunflowers. You'll like it."

Then, in all the wishing and wanting, there was Leah, telling her about sunflowers and making her a valentine. Olympia turned to wave and smile before she skipped past the grown-ups. Olympia bounced up the bus steps.

"Watch your step, girl," Miss Brinker warned.

"Yes, Miss Brinker," she said.

Scooting into *their* seat, hers and Leah's on the bus, she waved goodbye and watched as Leah tried to tell her something. Her hands cupped around her mouth.

"She didn't mean you." The words were shapes without sound.

Olympia thought that's what Leah had said and tried to believe her.

37. Winter Mud

It was a strange winter, with strange weather: hot when it should have been cold; wet when it should have been dry; thunderstorms when there should have been drizzle; corduroy jackets worn on Sunday and sweaters that wound up tied around a kid's waist on Wednesday. It made knowing what to wear tricky. It made Blarney, the Irish setter, paranoid.

Blarney didn't understand about winter rain and how it was possible for the sky to turn gray and pour for days without one single flash of lightning or clap of thunder. For Blarney, rain meant thunder, and thunder meant mind-gnawing, heart-exploding terror.

Not long after Miss Rhodes explained the worries of clean hair and lice to her mom, the sun came up, but didn't come out; it stayed hidden behind a grumpy wall of clouds. Rain or shine, the calf still had to be fed and his stall cleaned.

Leah hustled her way to the barn, hoping for a miracle, wanting the calf to be better, perkier. She watched as the first drips of rain on Blarney's boney, red head made him stop, whine, and bolt back to the house. His terror sent him crashing toward their carport. When he hit the carport cement he slipped, knocking over a row of garbage cans. The metal cans lost their lids. One lid rolled across the carport and smacked into the family station wagon. It fell to the ground like a top, spinning slower and slower and finally spinning down. The sound sent Blarney into a blind, foaming panic. He barked, bit, and yowled his terror.

He raced back out into the rain, away from the thundering noise, away from the house, across a muddy yard, towards the barn.

"Stop, Blarney, stop!" Leah shouted, but he was beyond hearing.

In the barn he ran in circles, tipping over a wheelbarrow full of manure, and tried to squeeze into the calf's pen, but got a head butt for his trouble. That head butt was the most Apollo the Calf had moved all day.

Manure, hay, and fear covered the wet dog. A pitchfork toppled onto him from the corner of the calf pen. It was like he thought that the pitchfork was a bolt of lightning let loose in the barn. Blarney ran back to the house.

Leah's mom opened the door, stuck her head out, and yelled, "Leah, what's happening out here?"

Blarney, caked and covered in filth, slammed past her through the open door, while her mother's screams reached all the way across the yard.

"Leah! Come. Get. This. Dog."

Leah could hear the ominous sound of furniture crashing over.

"Now!"

She raced through the rain back to the house in time to see Blarney making another muddy circuit around the kitchen table, and then running up the stairs to the bedrooms. Everything Blarney touched was streaked with mud and worse.

Her mom grabbed a broom. Leah bolted up the stairs after the dog.

She was just in time to see Blarney find Bobby's room and fling himself through the open door and onto a tower of Tinkertoys into the safest place he could find: Bobby's bed.

By the time Mom got to the bed to find the giant, quivering lump under the freshly washed sheets, she was crying. The lump whimpered. Leah's mom said a bad word and then cried some more. Bobby yelled about his smashed Tinkertoy project. Mom whacked at the lump. Blarney exploded from under the muddy sheets and retreated back the way he had come, mud still flying.

Mom started to strip sheets, sobbing and chanting.

"I hate this place. I hate this place. I hate that dog and I hate these people."

She stopped when she saw Leah staring.

"Don't just stand there. Help me." She didn't say it mean. It was just sad.

Leah left and followed a trail of sloppy paw prints to go and find a broom.

38. *Winter Ice*

After Valentine's Day, winter threatened to turn the orange grove next to the children's house into an ice sculpture. The frost report warned of a hard freeze. The grove workers had come early while the children were at school to set up the smudge pots, iron tubs full of oil or kerosene with tall stacks like chimneys. They stacked tires to burn. They would stay all night—feeding the fire, burning the rubber tires they had stacked at the edge of the orange grove, and lighting the smudge pots.

Their mother warned them about playing in the orange grove when the grove workers were there. The workers frightened her. The children could tell by the way she said she would punish them if they disobeyed her. The children could tell by the way she kept peeking through the kitchen curtains at the men. The men who were trying to keep the orange trees from frost damage.

At sunset the wind died.

The temperature dropped hour after hour.

At dinnertime the temperature was in the forties.

After the six o'clock news it dropped into the thirties.

Right before the children's bedtime, the mercury read twenty-nine degrees and the head grove worker, the boss man, ordered the crews to light the smudge pots and set the tires on fire.

Fire roared out of the top of the pots. Smoke rolled over the trees. The workers scurried back and forth through the trees, watching the fires. Black choking smoke rolled off of the burning tires. It wasn't the fires that were supposed to save the trees; it was the smoke. The grove workers hoped the cloud over the trees would hold the heat in like a blanket.

The smudge pot fires filled the grove with globes of light shaped like mushrooms, as clouds of oily smoke drifted. Shadows grew and got long, thrown weirdly out of proportion by the mix of flame and smoke. The grove workers hurried from pot to pot. Their scurrying bodies cast ten-foot-tall stick figure shadows against the backdrop of orange trees grown heavy and drooping with fruit. The shadow men flopped their way through the trees like scarecrows. Their arms folded and unfolded like a spider's legs weaving webs out of black fog. Some of the shadow men had huge, swollen, bubble-headed shadows—because of their big, round hair.

The children could see the lurching, black

shadows when they went to the barn to check on the sick baby calf, and later from their bedroom windows when they were getting ready to go to bed.

Transformed, the orange grove came alive with the spidery shadows that quivered under a sky filled with ice. The men danced to an ugly, jittery music, their faces growing blacker and blacker in the greasy soot of the smudge pot fires.

Seeing it gave the children nightmares.

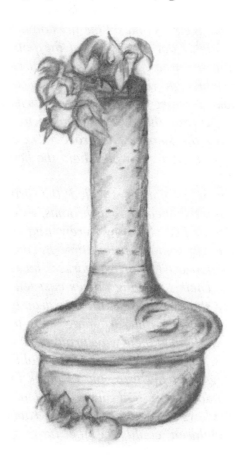

39. Winter Calm

Worried about a hard freeze, the children put a blanket on the calf early in the evening, tying it on with the twine from the hay bales. It wasn't hard to do that now because the calf had grown so much calmer. That's what they called the calf's stillness—calm. He didn't bounce or jump around any more. He was just quiet—too quiet.

A local rancher, Mr. Westly, with grease smears on his jeans, came to look at their baby calf after Dad told Mom to call him. The rancher was not gentle. He pulled the calf to its feet, poking and prodding and pulling the calf's tail so he could look at the calf's bottom. The little calf bawled and cried, but the rancher did not care. He just squatted down in the pen and watched when the calf lifted its tail again and again to poop and poop.

Mr. Westly didn't ask what they had named the calf or if they'd fallen in love.

Putting a piece of clean straw in his mouth, he waved sadly at the flies that landed on his face. He watched without talking while Leah and her brother hung on the fence with their chins propped on the top board.

Their mom waited right outside the barn door because of her allergies while the farmer waved flies away. She kept her arms wrapped around her middle. She wore a huge sweater that made her look like a giant, fuzzy caterpillar, and she frowned like the caterpillar might frown from *Alice in Wonderland.*

"You know a lot of these orphan calves get pretty sick, Mrs. Breck. And a lot of them don't make it."

He stood up and kicked at a pile of soiled hay. The calf sneezed and the blanket slipped to one side. Bobby tried to straighten the blanket, but it slipped farther to one side.

"Baby calves are better when they can suck their mom's milk."

"What's wrong with it?"

"Well, it has got the scours, for sure. It's diarrhea, but it can get so bad that they do not . . ."

Mom waved her hands in a rush to stop whatever he was going to say, but Leah, who was becoming an expert at decoding grown-up talk, knew what he meant.

They died—a lot. Baby calves died a lot without their moms.

"You need scours medicine."

"We're doing that," she said. "We've been doing that."

Mom glanced at her watch.

"Well, he needs a bottle in two more hours . . ."

The rancher looked puzzled.

"Why two hours?"

"Babies eat every two hours. Right?"

Mr. Westly sighed and pushed his ball cap back away from his face to the back of his head. He scratched his forehead. Leah could see that his fingernails were black with grease and dirt, and the wrinkles of his face had grime in them.

He sighed again.

"Maybe human babies, but calves drink in the

morning and in the evening. That's why dairy cows get milked two times a day. You're working way too hard about this."

Mom looked so relieved, Leah felt sad. She hadn't realized how much her mom had been doing while she and her brother slept. Leah pressed her cheek against the scruffy wood of the fence and tried to blink back tears.

Glancing at Leah, Mr. Westly tried to be reassuring.

"Keep giving him the medicine and feed him only twice a day, and maybe he'll be fine."

He patted her head. His hand was heavy and hurt.

She wanted to tell the farmer that the calf wouldn't drink even two times a day now; he hardly drank anything at all. But she was too shy, and he didn't ask.

"It'll be fine. Sure, fine."

The calf lifted its tail again and shot a bubbly stream of diarrhea into the hay, but it didn't cry. Then he flopped back down in the hay. The blanket they'd tied around his middle twisted into a dirty lump.

40. Too Cold

When the temperature drops to twenty-five degrees Fahrenheit, there is nothing anyone can do to save an orange grove.

Next to Bobby and Leah's house, the orange grove died in the cold and nothing the men burned could keep the trees from becoming too cold for too long, and so the grafted branches died right down to the trunks.

The fruit on the trees was ruined when the water inside froze, rupturing the cell sacks. The oranges would shrivel and dry up.

The burning tires and the smudge pot fires hadn't saved anything.

41. The Happiest Color

On the way to school in the morning, the bus picked up Leah first. Leah, who always made sure to be sitting in *their* seat, was always waiting for Olympia. Their seat, in the second row on the right side of the bus, was the one with the foggy spot shaped like a penguin in the window glass. There was a tear in the green plastic of the bench seat.

Olympia made sure to avoid the rip in the seat when she slid in to sit down next to Leah. The edges of the rip scratched the back of her knees where her pleated skirt had gotten too short. Granny Mac grumbled that Olympia grew faster than collards in springtime. Granny always said that it was harder to keep Olympia in clothes than to keep shoes on a cat. But no matter how much Olympia grew, Leah grew exactly the same, and when they sat together and their legs dangled, they always matched. In that leftover row in the front of the school bus saved for all the kids too small or too different, they sat together, everyday, swinging their legs back and forth, their white lace ankle socks still the same.

Olympia loved how much they matched.

The morning after the freeze, she sat next to Leah with a jump and a wiggle. She didn't bother saying good morning. She didn't have to.

"Did you ask?"

Leah nodded her head and grabbed Olympia's hand.

"She says she's asking my dad, and I showed her where you lived." The bus rumbled away from Olympia's tiny home, balancing on cement blocks like a stilt walker.

"That's good. Is that what moms say? That she's thinking about it and asking your dad?"

"Maybe, I guess. My mom does."

"Because my Granny Mac mostly says no or yes, and that's all. She doesn't think about it; she just knows."

"Maybe, that's what my mom always says." Leah shrugged. "I brought you a present."

Olympia wriggled back against the stiff green seat with butterfly feelers in her stomach. Leah pulled a round smiley face pin out of her pencil box. She pushed it into Olympia's hand.

"I think yellow is the color of happy."

"Like sunflowers."

Olympia liked yellow. Her bedroom was plain, the curtains and bedspread every kind of color and pattern stitched together by her grandmother with her clever needle, all of it made out of the leftover rags and worn-out scraps of Olympia's growing up. That's how she liked to think of the quilted curtains and bedspread.

"I think patchwork is the happiest color."

"What color is that?" A little wrinkle appeared between Leah's eyes when she frowned.

Olympia didn't know how to explain patchwork. She didn't try; she hurried to reassure Leah.

"But yellow is the happiest smile color, and I want to wear it right now."

It's all she could think of to say, to try to tell Leah how it felt to have someone like her waiting every morning in the seat with the penguin smudge in the window.

"I'll give you something back tomorrow when you come on the bus."

"No, you can't."

Olympia pried the pin open. She pricked her finger on the sharp point.

"Sure I will," she said, wiping the tiny drop of blood on her skirt.

"Nope, my mom is going to drive me to school tomorrow. She's going to drive me to school all the time from now on."

The bus bounced across the bump under the traffic light on Highway 46—going too fast. The children gasped and giggled at being thrown in the air out of their seats. It made Olympia feel like the time she'd fallen off the swing at recess and landed facedown in the dirt. It made her stomach feel like it had come unhooked from the rest of her body and was still hanging in the air.

"But why? Do you have to go to that dentist again?"

Leah shrugged and frowned.

"I . . . no. She just said she'd be driving us in

the car," Leah said. "Maybe it's so my brother will do better at school or something."

At first, what Leah was telling Olympia seemed silly. Then she realized no one would be waiting for her tomorrow morning in the seat with the rip and the foggy penguin in the window.

Olympia polished the happy face with the edge of her skirt.

"I like this present, but I don't want you to drive to school with your mom."

"I know."

"But you'll be at school like always, right?"

Leah looked over at Olympia and smiled. Leah's face was like the happy face pin, except her cheeks weren't yellow; they were pink under her freckles. They made Olympia think of stars—those freckles on Leah's face.

If I had to pick one color, I wish my bedroom could be pink. There would be pink clouds and pink candy and pink stars on the walls and bed and floor, because pink's my favorite color. Pink like Leah's cheeks.

42. Down

Two days after Leah stopped riding on the bus back and forth to school, the calf went down and only stood up when the children dragged him up onto his feet.

Mom called Dr. Dunn, the veterinarian, but he had to come all the way from Titusville and couldn't get there until the next day. After school,

Leah and her brother had gone to sit with the baby calf so he wouldn't be lonely or scared.

"Daddy would know what to do," Bobby said. He ran his hand down one still brown leg.

Leah didn't answer her brother. The calf's ear twitched. She brushed away a fly that tickled his ear. He lay in the hay with his head down now, and she had to pick his head up and pull it onto her lap.

"We should stop fighting about his name and pick one, I think."

"Daddy would know what to call him," her brother said.

"No, he wouldn't."

"Yes, he would."

"No, because Daddy's not here and that means he couldn't know what to call him because he's too busy being somewhere else."

Her brother frowned and pulled his ball cap down over his eyes.

Leah felt for the hard knots where horns would grow on the calf's head, wondering what Dad would do differently if he had been here. She looked at her brother, wanting to believe the way he did. She felt a little bit sorry for him. He was just a kid, after all.

They both reached out to pat the calf, concentrating on the small patches of skin under their hands and avoiding looking at the calf's side, which barely moved. Sometimes Leah had to stare for a long time to convince herself he was still breathing at all.

43. The Name of Things

Leah worked hard to avoid the brussels sprouts on her plate. Mom called them "baby cabbages." Whatever Mom called them, they were disgusting.

"Eat your dinner," Mom said, sitting at the end of the dining room table.

Leah's brother sat across the table, the better to stick his tongue out at her with half-chewed food on it. Dad's chair was still empty. Because the room was paneled in a dark oak and had heavy open-beamed ceilings, the room, like all the rooms in their house, stayed dark.

Leah pushed brussels sprouts around the rim of her plate with a fork.

"Eat," her mother repeated.

She pushed the sprouts faster, and one rolled off her plate. It wobbled across the table and bumped the rim of her brother's plate.

She reached across the table to catch it.

"Oops."

Her brother jumped on a reason to complain.

"Leah's not eating."

Mom frowned him down.

"And you're not eating either. Hush and eat."

Forks clinked against dishes. Her brother started to pile mashed potatoes over his vegetables. The refrigerator hummed softly in the kitchen.

Leah wondered if they would have brussels sprouts when Olympia got to spend the night. She wrinkled her nose up.

"Mom, can we have fried chicken when Olympia spends the night? And green beans, and not . . . these ugly things?"

Bobby jumped out of his chair, hopping up and down. He forgot his mashed potato mountain long enough to dance and hop around the table. Holding a spoon in his hand, he pointed at his sister.

"Why does Leah get to have a friend over?" He smacked at his potato mountain with the spoon when he danced by his plate.

"You need to stop, right now." Her mother's voice sounded like it was tied up with a rope. It sounded like she had all her attention on her brother, but when she glanced at her mother, Leah saw that her mom was looking over at her, without blinking. Her throat felt too full, suddenly. Still, she had to have an answer—finally. She had to know.

"Can we have my favorite?"

"That girl Olympia," Mother held her fork in her hand like a magic wand, "is she the girl you were sitting with at school? On the steps?"

"Sure. She's the smartest girl in my class."

Her brother slapped at his potatoes, whining. He balanced on the edge of his seat. Potatoes flicked from his spoon onto the tabletop.

"Not fair."

"She's one of those kids that lives down Spring Hill Road." It wasn't a question. "Is that right?"

It was the way she said *one of those kids* that did it. A fist closed in Leah's stomach, making a hard, knuckled lump. All she could do was nod her head.

"Did you remember to ask Dad?" Leah knew

she had, remembering her mother's voice—one half of a phone conversation—the smaller half. Her mother only saying, "Yes," "No," "I understand," and "Of course, dear."

She watched her mother's shoulders tighten, her mother's chin lift and wobble.

"He said no, Leah. She's not to come to this house."

Bobby looked at his sister; even he was surprised. Leah felt sick.

"But," her voice felt rusty, "why?"

Her mother wiped at the plops of mashed potatoes next to her brother's plate, not looking at either one of them.

"Because," she said, pausing.

Leah was afraid that her mother was done talking, leaving her with one of those grown-up explanations that never meant anything or explained anything or fixed anything. Disappointment and confusion threatened to swamp her.

"Because your father wouldn't be comfortable with a girl like that here, not from Spring Hill Road, because your father's from West Virginia."

Why were they talking about places on a map?

"But you said a long time ago that she could. Don't you remember?"

Her mother's voice sounded a warning like a flashing yellow light in the room.

"Leah."

"But you said."

"Your father said, 'No' and that means no."

"Mom!" Leah wanted to say, *"Answer me,"* *"Explain this,"* *"Help me,"* *"Stop this,"* but it came

123

out as "Mom, please!"

"Because of Grandma Breck."

Everything her mother said made it worse.

Her brother, over his surprise, wanted to celebrate Leah's defeat. He started to hum under his breath—nothing recognizable, nothing punishable—just a dull, low, nasty chant.

Mom snapped at him.

"Sit down and eat."

"I can't. I need ketchup."

"Leah, get your brother some ketchup."

At first, she couldn't understand the instruction. It was as incomprehensible as Grandma Breck's name being used as an explanation as to why Olympia could not come to their house.

"Go. Get the ketchup."

She got up, opened the refrigerator, and stared at the jumble inside. A pool of light washed over her hands and face. The hard lump in her stomach melted and poured out of her eyes. It got hard to see.

"I can't find it."

"Look harder."

"I . . . can't . . . find . . . anything," Leah said, hiccupping.

A chair cracked against the floor behind her. Someone had pushed against a chair so hard it had fallen over.

"It's in there, just look."

Leah sniffed, wanting to wipe her nose on her sleeve.

"I can't . . ."

Mom grabbed her by the shoulders and spun

Leah around. The refrigerator light fell on her mom's face and turned it a dull yellow. It made her look ill.

"Because, that girl can't come to this house . . . because there was a sign outside of the town where he grew up that said, *Nigger, if you can read this— run! If you can't read this—run anyway.* Because he grew up that way . . . because it's his way, and it was Grandmother Breck's way . . . because she's not white. That's why. And that's an ugly word, Leah, and you made me say it."

She let Leah go and pushed past her to shove and shuffle things around inside the refrigerator.

"Oh look, I found it. It's right here in front of your face."

She carried the ketchup into the dining room, expecting Leah to follow.

"Come and eat your baby cabbages."

Brussels sprouts, they're called brussels sprouts, Leah thought, and then leaned her cheek against the closed door of the refrigerator. She could see the frilly edge of the valentine she'd made for her mom with *Be My Valentine* spelled out in glue and glitter. Leah's mom had taped it up. It was exactly like the valentine she'd made for Olympia. She read the words in silver glitter, but they didn't make any sense to her, anymore than the words in her head made sense. The words that her mother had put there, her father's words—words that were somehow her grandmother's way.

Leah whispered under her breath, "But that sign wasn't about Olympia. They didn't mean her.

44. *Blasted*

After the freeze, the oranges went unpicked. The fruit hung, unwanted and ruined—not fit to eat, not worth picking even for the orange juice factories. The trees looked sandblasted. Their limbs were skeletal, all hard lines and joints, their silhouettes fragile. Blasted limbs stood out against the murk of winter skies.

Miss Lockerbee didn't wait for the threat of frost to pass; the grove was pruned immediately. The grove workers came to lop and chop and cut the dead wood off to keep the trees from going wild, back to its rootstock—back to sour fruit. They tried to save the trees before it was too late.

For most of the oranges, it was already too late. The cold had come too hard and stayed too long.

Many of the oldest trees, already weakened by age and disease, did not survive at all. The grove workers ignored the dead trees, moving on to the ones that might come back in the spring. They used handsaws to cut away the ruined parts of the orange trees.

A dump truck came to haul away the dead wood. The orange trees disappeared limb by limb and branch by branch, but some of the brush got piled up way in the back along the back boundary of the orange trees in twisted, tangled heaps. Forgotten. The dump truck driver had been worried about getting stuck in the soft sugar sand at the back of the grove and had pretended he never saw the piles stacked in the back; he abandoned them.

Overnight, the orange grove became a strange place, a thin place.

The boy mourned for his lost fortress beyond the piles of forgotten cuttings behind the trees. The girl did not look at the orange grove; it was too shocking. The long dirt rows between the naked pruned trees were raw, like claw marks left in the ground by some great dragon. She ignored looking. She ignored seeing. She pretended she did not care that so much had died in the cold.

45. Whispering

Leah stood in front of her closet mirror, hating the way her knee socks made her knees look like lumpy knots. She hated the way her elbows matched her knees, thin and white and freckled. She pulled her smiley face sweatshirt over her arms, happy to watch her elbows disappear into the heavy sleeves. Her lips hurt; they were chapped. She pulled at a curl of skin at the edge of her mouth. Ouch! It hurt enough to make her eyes smart with tears. She focused on her sore mouth, convincing herself that if she started to cry it would be because of her chapped mouth.

Leah watched her mouth move as she practiced what she was going to say to Olympia today. It had to be today. Her mouth moved but no sounds came out. It was like her voice had been stolen in the night. Her lips moved, but there was the sound of nothing, of fear. She cleared her throat and forced herself to make sounds.

"Olympia, my dad says that you can't come to my house." Her voice sounded sharp like paper tearing. She tried again.

"Olympia, my dad doesn't want you inside our house." Leah needed to make Olympia understand. Leah stared hard at her chapped mouth.

"Olympia, my mom and dad won't let you come to my house because of that sign with bad words on it when my dad was a little boy. I don't know why."

But that was a lie. In the mirror, Leah watched her mouth lie. She knew why they wouldn't let Olympia spend the night, and in a place inside, a deep place that Leah had not known existed, a tiny worm had started nibbling at the shadows in her head, the shadows and the memories and the worries.

Maybe it's better this way, the worm whispered, while it ate and ate and grew and grew.

Leah pulled at another tiny curl of skin from her lip. It made her mouth bleed. Licking at the blood, she concentrated on the stinging burn. She tried to ignore the worm and its whispering.

46. Meatloaf and Green Beans

Wednesday was meatloaf and green bean day in the tiny cafeteria at Evegan Elementary. The green beans were fresh and cooked with hunks of bacon fat, and the meatloaf was homemade. It was one of Olympia and Leah's favorite days because they both loved meatloaf, and Olympia always traded her green beans for Leah's roll.

Steam from the bubbling pots misted the windows, making the room cozy warm in the winter. The lunch ladies baked homemade yeast rolls every morning. They got to school at four so the bread dough would have time to rise. The smell of yeast lingered like perfume all day long. The cafeteria was like somebody's kitchen at home, but with better and more food.

Wednesday had a special smell all its own. Wednesday smelled like homemade rolls and felt as comforting as steam on the inside of a window on an icy winter day.

47. Lunchroom

There was time to talk to each other at lunch, not much, but some. Even on Meatloaf Wednesdays, talk and talking were more important than homemade rolls or fresh green beans, especially when worries at home had tipped over and spilled out all over the floor like a wheelbarrow full of manure.

Leah gave Olympia her roll without asking to trade for the green beans. She started pushing the green beans she already had around with her fork.

"Don't you want my beans?" Olympia tipped her plate toward Leah. "I got a piece of bacon with mine. You can have it." She pushed her plate closer, splashing green bean juice on the table between them.

Leah hardly noticed the spill or her friend's offer. She dropped her fork and folded her hands in her lap.

"Don't you?"

"Nope . . . not today."

"Come on. You love these beans; they're your favorite. Granny Mac always has green beans for dinner. They're from the garden. I'm used to 'em."

Leah smiled at her folded hands. She shook her head.

"I know, but my stomach feels bad."

"My granny can fix that. She can fix anything. She's almost like a doctor." Olympia talked while she pushed forkfuls of meatloaf into her mouth. "You need my granny to fix you?"

That made Leah smile too, wishing she knew someone like Granny Mac who could fix everything; maybe she could fix the dread Leah felt about tomorrow and tomorrow and tomorrow and all the tomorrows after that.

"No, she can't fix me. But our baby calf is so sick. You know, the one I told you about—with your eyes and curly eyelashes."

Leah looked at her friend's eyes. Was anything as deep and dark and brown as they were? They made Leah think about all the warm, soothing moments they had together like when they held hands. It made her think of other soothing times: sitting on a grandma's lap, cuddling with a book, or finding a perfect hiding place, a secret place where Bobby couldn't find her when they played hide-

and-seek.

It was Olympia's turn to smile.

"When I spend the night, I am going to draw a picture of my sister, the baby cow."

"Brother, it's a boy," Leah corrected.

You can't see him. You can't see him ever.

But she couldn't say it, not yet. Leah tried to pretend that she would never have to say it.

Olympia laughed and that got her a frumpy look from the lunchroom teacher, who liked the cafeteria to be filled with the sounds of chewing and digesting and not too much laughing.

"What did you pick? What's your baby cow's name?"

Leah made a face.

"My dumb brother calls him Tank, but I've been thinking that I want to call him Apollo. Remember?"

"Apollo, that's good—like those gods who never die."

Hearing her friend say the name out loud made Leah remember how thin Apollo had gotten. He wasn't bright and shiny and strong like the pictures in the book about Greek myths. He wasn't even very brown anymore; his coat was dull and rough and dirty. Leah took a bite of her meatloaf. It was hard to swallow.

"He's sick."

Leah must have sounded extra sad. Olympia quit chewing. She patted her friend's hand.

"Mr. Westly said that he does have scours and that means his tummy is upset all the time."

"Well, I don't know about that, but I know my

Granny Mac will know all about such a thing. She knows about leaves and roots and sassafras and planting things under a full moon in springtime. She learns all that stuff from *The Farmer's Almanac.* Should I ask for medicine for Apollo?"

Olympia said it with such confidence that it made Leah feel better automatically, and for a moment she believed that it might help. That Granny Mac would know what to do, that her friend would come to her house to stay, that the world would always smell like yeast and homemade rolls, and that her stomach would never be upset.

Olympia peeked to make sure the lunchroom ladies weren't watching and then scooped her green beans onto Leah's plate. It hurt the lunch ladies' feelings when the kids didn't eat every bit of their own food. Leah wanted to try and eat the green beans now and took a bite.

Olympia winked at Leah.

"When I come to spend the night, I'll bring something from my granny to fix up my baby brother. Do you think your mom will make meatloaf or what?"

She pushed Leah's puffy yeast roll into her mouth, smiling around the mouthful. She had a lot of teeth. They looked strong and too white in her black face.

Dark, Leah realized; black. Her face was so dark compared to the white, puffy roll.

Olympia looked just like those raggedy scarecrows in the orange grove whose shadows had danced through the fires. Just like them, and Leah's dad didn't like that.

Leah lost her appetite for Olympia's extra green beans.

48. Brussels Sprouts and Chalk

To Leah, that Wednesday smelled like the black fog rolling over an orange grove from an oily fire, and it tasted like brussels sprouts and chalk dust.

49. Looking

Olympia loved Evegan Elementary and the important things the students had to practice.

They had to practice hiding under their desks if Russians fired missiles at the school. Olympia didn't think the Russians would shoot bombs at their school but, maybe, because the space rockets at the Cape were so close a bomb might fall on them by accident.

When Mrs. Ward gave the signal, everyone was supposed to crawl underneath their desks and cover up their heads. Mrs. Ward was very serious when she practiced giving the signal. Still, Olympia found it hard not to giggle when somebody bumped their head and yelled, "Ouch."

Another thing to practice was walking quickly out of school in an orderly fashion for fire drills. Olympia loved fire drill day. It felt like a tiny day off from school. The Evegan Volunteer Fire Department, newly formed and proud of their important role in the community, always brought a fire engine for the first and second graders to climb on. The firemen talked about fire safety and how to dial zero to talk to the operator if anyone needed to report a fire, or where they should write down the fire department's phone number.

During a fire drill, Olympia and Leah always walked out of the school straight to the chain-link fence. They were supposed to grab the fence with one hand and wait for the teachers to count their heads. The faster they walked out, the sooner they could begin talking and goofing around.

Everyone had a buddy for fire drill day. At first, Olympia's buddy had been a boy named Eddie, but he had refused to hold hands with her, so Mrs. Ward had made Leah Olympia's buddy, which was a wonderful bit of luck.

The fire alarm went off right after lunch, right after meatloaf and green beans. Everyone had been working on a worksheet about stars and planets. It was very important to understand about space if they were going to grow up and beat the Russians to the moon and all the rest of those planets—maybe even Pluto.

Olympia had wanted to ask about those stars. She wanted to know if other people wondered about them the way she did. Did other people feel as small as she did when she looked into the night sky? She imagined herself standing on the moon and looking at the earth. Would it be like a beautiful marble hanging in a black sky? She wanted to ask Leah what she thought about the stars.

Leah would have looked up at the night sky and

wondered about the stars. She was that kind of person. Leah would feel how magical the moon looked when it hung above their heads, close enough to be touched, close enough to be reflected in a pair of emerald eyes, Leah's eyes, the same way moonlight moved over the surface of a pond.

When the fire alarm rang, Leah had been staring out of the window, but she couldn't see any stars, not even the big one that was supposed to rule the day. The sky was winter gray, hanging low and heavy like wet yarn over the basketball court. The sound of the alarm made Leah clench her fists. She glanced back at Olympia who was already smiling at her.

Olympia's smile was too bright in her black face. Why doesn't she have freckles like me? Leah wondered. Not fair.

Mrs. Ward looked annoyed at the sound of the alarm.

"All right students, just leave everything exactly like it is, and line up and take your buddy by the hand. That means you two, John T. and Robert. You won't die. Now hold hands."

Olympia was at Leah's desk before Leah could put down her pencil.

"Come on, buddy," she laughed. Olympia was always laughing.

Leah could tell Mrs. Ward wanted this silly fire drill over in a hurry, so they could get back to their desks and finish their work.

"And no talking please."

Olympia grabbed Leah's hand. Leah pulled her hand out of Olympia's and wiped it against the smiley face on her sweatshirt.

"Sorry," Leah whispered. "My hand's all sweaty."

"Quiet, please."

Olympia shrugged, grabbed Leah's hand again, and squeezed it tight.

Mrs. Ward's class filed out into the hallway, behind Mrs. Beed's fifth grade class. Big kids bunched up and pushed back against the smaller kids. Some of the bigger boys started to push the younger ones.

Wayne wandered out of the boy's bathroom and walked near Leah. He punched her in the arm. She staggered into Olympia. Rhonda made a fist and waved it at Wayne.

Principal Jonas waded between the two classes like a giant, snapping his fingers at the older kids.

"Be sure and use the handrail when you walk down the steps, and keep moving; no more broken arms, thank you."

Mrs. Ward kept her class moving, down the steps to their designated area, away from the fifth graders. Their spot was beyond the new kindergarten portable next to the chain-link fence. Some of the kids started to sit down on the ground next to the fence, huddling up like chickens under the cold, damp day.

Mrs. Ward hissed at the kids sitting down.

"Stand up. We're not going to be out here long enough to get comfortable. Young man, stop that."

She stomped off in the direction of a boy name Marcus, who had started to climb the fence to be funny.

Leah let Olympia pull her next to the trunk of an oak tree that grew just inside the fence. The trunk was big and old and it blocked out the school if you stood in just the right spot. Its roots grew in twists and turns and lumps, and it was fun to imagine you were lost in an enchanted wood when you stood next to it.

Olympia didn't wait to start talking. Leah knew she wouldn't.

"Did your mom . . .?"

Leah didn't want to hear the end of the sentence. She didn't want to hear the question mark at the end of the sentence. She rubbed at her sore mouth and tried pretending something, anything, but she couldn't. She couldn't pretend hard enough to make the question go away. She could hear Olympia still talking, still asking about Friday night.

Leah's answer came out in a frog croak.

"You can't."

Olympia didn't stop asking. The questions just changed.

"But why not? Not now, but when? When can I come?"

Leah had practiced more words to explain, but they had all run away, and the only words left were the bad ones.

"You just can't."

Leah put her hands over her ears. She knew that Olympia was still talking, but Leah didn't have any answers that made sense. The questions kept getting louder. She turned to look at the trunk of the tree. Its craggy surface looked like a foreign planet

where thousands of ants crawled here and there—
going places, looking for something. The ants made
Leah think about cootie bugs. Were cooties like
that? Crawling here and there in a person's hair?

Leah could hear her name being repeated over
and over again.

Finally, Olympia grabbed Leah by the
shoulders and shook her.

50. The Color of Ugly

It was the first time Olympia had ever put her
hands on her friend like that; she felt so frustrated
and impatient. It was the first time Olympia noticed
the way Leah's cheeks got ugly, red blotches when
she cried; red blobs of color in her too white face.
Her eyes were red rimmed. They looked raw. They
looked ugly.

"They said you can't come over—ever," Leah
said.

"But why?"

The answer was already in Leah's eyes.
Olympia could see it. Leah shook her head; it was a
silly pointless movement. She shrugged, her face
crumpling up even more. Her freckles stood out
against her skin like fly specks.

Several kids wandered over to stand behind the
tree—sensing drama. Rhonda stood on the other
side of the oak tree, peeking around the hard curve
of the trunk at them. Wayne stood next to the fence
behind them, watching with a smirk, eavesdropping
like a bat hanging upside down in a cave.

"Because . . . my dad said things about people who live where you do."

Wayne stepped close to Olympia; he kept sneaking looks to see if any teachers were listening.

"Because you're purple tongued and red gummed, and that means you're poison," Wayne said. He looked like he wanted to clap or jump for joy.

Rhonda gasped when she heard what Wayne had said.

Olympia didn't have enough breath in her lungs to gasp or cry. Instead of air, she felt like her body was filled with sand. She couldn't move or make a sound. Leah only stared, sniffing quietly.

It was Rhonda who finally moved. Walking over to Wayne, she pushed him.

He stumbled back against the oak tree and then into a fire ant hill. The fire ants boiled out of the ground. Wayne yelped and scrambled away on his hands and knees before the ants could find him. He jumped up brushing at the dozens of ants on his legs.

Everyone was looking at Olympia anyway, even with the strange sight of Wayne crawling away like a hermit crab. She could feel all their eyes on her. No one even looked at Rhonda. They were all watching her still holding Leah by the shoulders.

Wayne's words felt like the stings of all those tiny, hidden ants that lived in the tree bark and under the ground. She looked at Leah, who hadn't said anything, who hadn't defended her or objected, who stood with her head down—miserable and afraid—and then her friend did a horrible thing, more horrible than even Wayne's words.

Leah looked up, right at her, but she didn't look at her face. Leah looked at Olympia's hair—searching—and Olympia knew what she was looking for.

It was worse than being slapped, that look, worse than the words. She shook Leah harder to stop her from looking.

"And you . . . you're just a damned, silly honkey girl—a whitey cracker. That's what my daddy said, and he's right. He knew it would be like this. I asked my granny too, and she told me not to be too sad when it happened. She knew you'd be a big 'fraidy cat, rednecked honkey. You know what my daddy says about white folks? That it's the ugliest things in the world that are white, like the bellies of fish and frogs. Like maggots. Ugly. Ugly."

Olympia felt the words gush out of her—the lumpy, stupid words—and watched as Leah's face turned whiter than the color of chalk dust under her splotchy, ugly freckles.

She pushed Leah away from her, blinking back hot tears, swallowing the burning lump in her throat.

Then the all-clear bell rang and the fire drill was over.

The whole class groaned as they lined up to their worksheets about space, and then after that there would be another sixty minutes of multiplication tables until the buses came to take everybody home. Everyone found their fire drill partners and filed back to their classroom.

Olympia didn't hold Leah's hand, but a lot of kids didn't bother to hold hands when they went back into school after the fire drill. It seemed more important to hold hands when you left the school than when you went back in.

Mrs. Ward didn't seem to notice or care.

51. Far Away Storms

Leah rode home in a dragging fog of misery. After the fire drill, Olympia hadn't looked at her, not even once. But Leah didn't want Olympia to look at her, too afraid that she'd see brown eyes filled up to the top with shiny wet tears.

Leah didn't want Olympia to look at her or say anything to her. Or call her names ever again. The names that made her feel like she'd been pushed out of the biggest orange tree in the world onto the hardest ground in the universe.

When Mom drove past the school bus on Spring Hill Road, Leah tried to see if Olympia was looking out of the window from their seat, their place on the bus, but no face pressed against the window—no one waved. Their seat looked empty.

The rest of the ride home was a watery blur, and then she saw Dr. Dunn waiting in the driveway. He leaned against his pickup truck with a stethoscope around his neck. Blarney sat next to the vet, panting hard, worried about something—maybe thunder only he could hear.

When Leah saw the veterinarian, she thought she might understand how Blarney dog felt when he

141

worried about storms too far away for anyone else to hear.

Leah's mother walked straight over to Dr. Dunn and shook his hand. The vet looked at the ground, kicking at the dirt while he talked. Leah watched her mother's shoulders pinch up tight to her ears. It was not a happy talk, Leah could tell.

Watching them made Leah remember that moment next to the chain-link fence at school when she'd felt like she had fallen to earth like a burning star. She went over it and over it in her head. The way the air had smelled like winter. The way Olympia's fingers had bitten into the bones of her shoulders. The way her heart had felt when it had split apart and all the air in her body had poured out into the dirt.

Leah didn't wait to hear what the grown-ups were saying. She opened the station wagon door on the opposite side from where they were talking and slipped out. She already knew what Dr. Dunn was telling Mom. But she wanted to see for herself; she needed to see for herself.

Sunshine poured across the hay, making a soft blanket of light inside the calf's pen. The pen looked empty, at first. Leah started to hope—a little bit. Maybe, maybe, Dr. Dunn had been able to save him. She poked her head between the wooden boards of the pen.

The sun made her eyes water. When she could focus in the glare, she saw the calf. He was curved against the back wall of the pen, like a question mark, but the question had been asked and answered. His eyes were open and empty as if all the light in them had been switched off. A fly buzzed and landed on the calf's open eye.

She heard Mr. Westly's voice in her head saying that orphan calves died all the time, got all kinds of things wrong with them. They were hard to raise because they got stuff from their mother's milk that they couldn't get from the powdered milk they put in the bottles.

She stared at what was left of him; his little body made her think of a popped balloon—all the air drained out of it. It was like a birthday balloon that had gotten away and drifted into some lonely field to fade away, the air seeping out of it slowly, bit by bit.

She remembered another voice.

We raised orphan calves all the time when I was a boy, he had said. *It's a great experience for any kid.*

It made her mad, those voices—all those grown-up voices. She was glad when her brother came to stand next to her at the pen. He carried the calf's bottle on his shoulder like a baby. What a day for Bobby to remember that it was his turn to feed the calf. He dropped the bottle on the ground in the dirt.

"Is he dead, Leah?" her brother asked. "He looks like a pancake."

For a few minutes, neither of them said anything. She took his hand.

"We didn't give him a name," he said. "Not really."

"Sure we did," she said and squeezed his hand. "His name is Tank."

143

Bobby started to cry.

"I don't want him to be like a pancake," he said. He backed away, turned, and ran.

Leah picked up the bottle at her feet and walked out of the barn toward more of those grown-up voices that talked and talked, back and forth. Bobby ran toward the house, and Blarney raced after him.

Dr. Dunn and Mom didn't notice when she slipped into the edge of their conversation.

"These dairy calves just don't get their mother's immunities. I'm sorry, but when they go down they go pretty fast. I was out in the area and thought I'd check."

Her mother sounded angry when it was her turn.

"My husband talked about it being easy enough."

"Well, that surprises me a little bit. You said that he grew up on a dairy farm?"

Then she sounded unsure.

"A dairy farm or something like that. He talks about it all the time, but I think that he was a very little boy and might not be remembering it right. This was an expensive experiment, otherwise."

Dr. Dunn finally noticed Leah standing behind her mom. He stepped past her mother, squatted down, and looked Leah in the face.

"I'm sorry about your little calf."

Leah didn't want him to be sorry. Leah wanted him to say something that helped or made a difference.

"Why? Why did he die?"

He started to say something plain and simple for a kid, she could tell. She watched him try to find easy words that wouldn't hurt too much, but when he looked at her he must have seen something in her face that made him stop.

"He had an infection in his lungs—pneumonia. It's hard to know what caused that, maybe germs."

"But my dad said it would be all right."

"I know."

Leah wanted Dr. Dunn to understand why she was sad.

"I'm afraid he'll want us to try again, and he'll get another one. My dad will, but I don't want to. It's too hard—when they die."

He lifted the bottle out of Leah's arms, and Mom made a motion to take the bottle from Dr. Dunn, but he stopped her.

"Show me something." He looked at Leah. "Show me; how high did you hold the bottle when you fed your calf?"

Leah stood up straight, took the bottle and held it out in front of her with two hands. She couldn't hold it for very long. She wasn't strong enough.

"Like this, but it's heavy, so I leaned it on the fence." She lowered the heavy bottle.

The vet looked down between his knees and grabbed a piece of grass, pulling it out of its sheath; it squeaked. He chewed on it and then looked over at her mother.

"Leah, show me where a momma cow's udders are."

But she didn't know what he wanted her to do.

He held his hand next to Leah's knees.

"Way down here. Now, where were you holding that bottle?"

"Up here." She showed him again. But when her arms were straight out they started to shake.

He took the bottle from her and held it low, near his knees.

"The baby cow, when he drinks from his mom's udders, has to reach down and lower his head, so that it gets a nice U-shape bend in its neck." He drew a *U* in the dirt with his finger. "That's the way it's supposed to be; when you hold the bottle too high, the calf's neck isn't bent. It's straight like a ramp, and the milk doesn't all go into the cow's tummy. Some of it runs straight into its lungs and they fill up . . ."

Leah's mother made a harsh sound—like a fingernail breaking against a chalkboard.

Dr. Dunn ignored Mom and looked straight at Leah.

"They drown in milk."

He stood up and looked at her mother.

"When your husband wants to play farmer again, you might want to pass the word on." He held the bottle out to Leah.

She looked at it. The milk had started to separate—watery at the top, with thick chunks at the bottom—ruined.

"Drowned." She said the word with a kind of wonder. "He didn't have a name yet. Not really. I called him one thing, but Bobby wanted . . . " She couldn't remember what she was going to say about what her little brother wanted.

Mom took the bottle from Doctor Dunn.

"Leah, it's not your fault."

"No," she said. "Okay. It's not."

Dr. Dunn patted her shoulder and made stupid grown-up noises that were supposed to make her feel better. He sounded like a chicken. Her mom stood silent, holding the bottle of milk in front of her like it was filled with poison. The milk sloshed when she sighed, a yellow glop stuck on the nipple.

Leah shrugged away from Dr. Dunn's hand and his clucking noise.

She looked at him. "Stop making those silly sounds. They're stupid."

Her mom gasped.

"Leah, that was rude."

Dr. Dunn dropped his eyes and then looked at her with a sad look. He was still trying to make her feel better.

"It's okay, Mrs. Breck, Leah's right. I couldn't be more sorry; you only did what you were told. But you should listen to your mom; she's right. It's not your fault."

She wanted to nod, but she could only shake her head from side to side. She didn't want them to try to make her feel better. She didn't want to feel better. Backing away from them and their stupid adult words and their stupid "sorry" faces, she tripped over a garden hose they had used to fill the calf's bucket. She fell onto her bottom and could smell hay and manure. It smelled like the dairy barn down here in the dirt, and she remembered the day they had brought the baby calf home.

She had to get away from that smell, from

147

them. She heard her name and then more pointless grown-up words.

"Leah, get up." Her mother sounded embarrassed, probably because of Dr. Dunn.

She flipped onto her knees and scrambled like a crab to her feet, and then started running.

52. The Other Side

Leah ran. She ran away from the smell and the memory and the voices and the impossible thoughts with clawed edges that banged around inside her head like birds in a cage, determined to get free or die. She pushed her way through the boards of the big paddock surrounding the barn, scrapping her backbone against the rough wood.

She pushed her way through the clumps of beard grass in the pasture. Dead and blasted by the freeze, the tufts still towered over Leah's head, rattling dead twigs. She ran along the meandering game trails through the weeds. Every trail led to the edge of the property and the barbed-wire fence separating their property from Miss Lockerbee's dead orange grove. Not going anywhere, not headed toward anything that she could name or explain, she ran hard.

She welcomed the bite of too little air in her lungs. It felt good to hurt this way, instead of the other pain, the pain that was inside her head. Too little air in her own lungs made her focus on her own hurting and not on the gurgling lungs of a dying calf.

At the edge of the field, Leah saw the sugar sand service road. She stopped running and looked at the barbed-wire fence, staring at the dividing line; the boundary line that measured the edges of the one place from the other. Before the world had turned to ice and sooty skies and the dancing of skeleton scarecrows, the fence had been a silly line. Now it felt like a wall—with a dead calf on one side and a dead world on the other.

She stood still, trying to find enough air to breathe. Her heart hammered at her ribs, demanding she listen to it.

For the first time, Leah looked at what was left of the orange grove. Before it had been frozen and they had come to chop it to pieces, it had seemed an endless place, as deep and wide and far as any two children might need.

Now, it looked ruined and naked. The mystery was hacked out of it, pulled down and stacked in tangled piles, dissolving away. Before it died, when the magic had still been in the trees, it had seemed like a story that never ended. Now it was five acres of magic reduced to sterile dirt rows, lined with amputated stumps.

Instead of squeezing through the strands of barbed wire without someone to help, Leah grabbed the top of a fence post and, careful to keep her feet on the strands of wire close to the sturdy post, she climbed. At the top of the fence, with one foot on the post and one on the topmost strand of wire, she balanced. For a minute, she felt like she might see all the way to that new museum in Orlando.

Without the screen of leaves and branches, she

could see from her side of the orange grove all the way to the far side. She jumped from the top of the fence into the white sand road and watched as cars raced by at the end of the naked rows. The cars were on Spring Hill Road, and she could stand right where she was at the edge of the two properties and see all the way to the end of the rows—no branches, no leaves, no clumps of weeds, no mystery, nothing to block her view.

She watched as the traffic on Spring Hill Road moved by, in an on-again, off-again stream. When she rode the bus to school, Spring Hill was a road she traveled down every day, excited to see Olympia, her friend, knowing that she lived there.

She could see Olympia's road. How could it be that Leah had not seen it? They were neighbors. She and Olympia lived close enough to walk to each other's house. How could she not have seen that they were neighbors?

The world had shrunk to two roads, Spring Hill Road and Old Town Road. At the corner of a ruined orange grove, the roads crisscrossed each other.

On Spring Hill Road, Olympia lived at the end of one of those wounded rows of trees in a wood-framed house on cement blocks with a burn barrel in the backyard. It was the yard where Granny Mac worked, burning leaves and waiting for Olympia to come home from school.

Leah stopped running away from the memory of brown eyes filled with moonlight that had turned to eyes made of mud where flies walked easily. She started running towards her friend, Olympia Crooms.

53. *First Grafts*

An orange grove blasted by cold and hacked back to the scars of its first grafts is like a broken, haunted place. Cold wind blows through the rows, carrying away topsoil in clouds. The wind makes a shrill screaming sound as it blasts its way through the naked limbs. Sand hisses and twists into dirt devils.

Sometimes a grove worker might paint the pruned end of the branches with black paint. It can look like black, dried blood. The paint is supposed to keep the tree sap in and the bugs out.

Along with the evergreen leaves of the citrus trees, all the secret dreaming places disappear under the scouring assault of the wind, and there's nowhere to hide. The wind blows the magic away in rolling, filthy clouds.

54. Crossing

It took Leah less than five minutes to run across the heavy, bare sand of the orange grove next to her house.

The first person she saw on the other side was a tiny woman bent at the waist, her hand wrapped around the handle of a hoe, her hair bundled into a frizzy lump on her neck. She was the color and texture of a palm trunk. Her hair was a tired white. She wore a shapeless blue dress, belted at the waist with an apron. The woman watched the fire in her burn barrel without moving, as still as a plant that grew out of the ground, even as the wind blew her skirt, puffing it up.

Leah ran to the edge of the yard and froze.

The old woman did not turn around or look at her. Leah was afraid of what would be in the old woman's face if she did turn around.

"I know you're there, child. You go ahead and call me Granny Mac."

"Yes ma'am. I mean Granny Mac, I've come for Olympia." Leah was afraid that she sounded too bossy. "I mean, I want to talk to Olympia, if it's okay."

Smoke poured out of the barrel into the darkening sky, shifting as the wind shifted. A storm rumbled somewhere near the coast, probably the storm Blarney had been worried about. The fire cracked and flared in the barrel.

"Well, good for you," she said, finally turning her head to look at Leah.

Leah's chest hurt, first from running and now from holding her breath, but then Granny Mac turned all the way around. The only thing she saw in the face of Olympia's grandmother was a gentle curiosity.

"You coulda come by here any other time, girl." She smiled a toothless grin. "I'm surprised you two girls didn't see a way through to each other sooner than this."

Leah was surprised too, and sad that she hadn't figured it out.

"I'm sorry." She didn't know what else to say.

"Sometimes it takes a while to see what's what, that's all. Olympia! Someone here for you; she's come a long way it seems."

Granny Mac pointed toward the white clapboard house and then turned back to her burn barrel.

55. The Smell of Rain

Olympia peeked through the lace curtain on the back door window. She heard Leah tell her grandmother that she had something that she needed to tell Olympia. Hearing Leah's voice made Olympia's heart pound again. This time it felt like a woodpecker in her chest, tapping away, looking for termites.

After pointing to the house, Granny Mac had gone back to her chores. Olympia watched Leah walk to the back of the house and wait at the bottom of the tired wooden steps that led up to the little porch.

Olympia didn't want to open the door right away; she wanted to make Leah wait. She was trying hard to stay mad and hurt, but she couldn't keep from peeking through a circle in the pattern of the lace curtain.

Leah must have seen her peeking. She made a tiny wave, and then climbed up the steps so she could knock on the door. She lifted her hand but, instead of knocking, Leah waved again. Olympia started to wave back before she could stop herself. It made her mad that she wanted to wave so easily. She grabbed the bottom of her T-shirt to keep her hand still.

Olympia opened the door.

"Where'd you come from?"

Leah smiled and shrugged, pointing her thumb back over her shoulder.

"Through the orange grove; it's not so very far at all."

Olympia looked passed Leah and Granny Mac at the naked orange trees.

"But I've always lived right here. Didn't you know? And anyway, I'm supposed to be mad at you. I want to be mad at you."

Leah flinched a little bit and started blinking hard, but Olympia didn't think it was the sun in her eyes, because the sky had filled up with heavy clouds, full of winter rain.

Granny Mac pulled herself up slowly by the railing of the steps. She came up behind Leah and patted her on the head. Then she patted Olympia on the head.

"I'm feeling a bit tired out today," she said, and then disappeared into the house. Her voice came from inside the house like a ghost.

"Olympia May Crooms, don't you be too quick to think your mad is bigger than someone's having their say. You girls stay close now, there's a storm coming on. I can smell the rain. Should I make some cookies for y'all?"

Surprised, Olympia looked at Leah and said, "That's something she doesn't ever do unless it's for a birthday."

"What? Smell rain coming?"

Olympia had to laugh in spite of wanting to

stay mad.

"No, Granny Mac can smell rain when the sun's still shining. It's her saying she'll make cookies. She never does that, except for special times." Olympia felt silly with Leah looking at her with her big eyes all shiny wet. "Are you here for a cookie or something?"

Leah shook her head and then the words started to gush out of her. She stood on the porch, her hands fisted at her sides.

"Olympia, I had to come here and tell you that he didn't know what to do. He didn't know. He told us what to do, but he was wrong, and I didn't know that he was wrong."

Gulping, she paused, trying to catch her breath, but then her face crumpled, and her nose started to run. She kept talking—the words a big jumble.

"We didn't . . . stop. We kept doing it . . . and then it died, but we didn't know why . . . and now we know, because Dr. Dunn told us."

Leah looked up at Olympia. She thought that Leah's eyes looked like they were full of broken things. Olympia threw open the door and threw her arms around Leah.

"Don't be sad," Olympia said. "Please don't."

Olympia could feel the bones in Leah's shoulders, and it reminded her of the fire drill, when she'd been so angry. It seemed a long time ago all of a sudden. She'd never realized how thin her friend was until that moment. To Olympia "her Leah" felt fragile, like one of the eggs from Granny Mac's speckled hens.

That's what she'd thought in her mind: *her*

Leah.

"Why are you so sad?"

"The baby calf drowned. Doctor Dunn just told us."

Olympia pulled her friend down onto the bottom step. She pressed her leg against Leah's leg, side by side—matching.

"What happened? Did the baby cow fall into a pond or something?"

Leah balled her hands back into fists and rested them on her knees.

"We did it."

"I don't know what you mean."

"We did it, because we listened to him . . ."

Olympia waited, confused.

"To my dad. He told us what to do, but he didn't know what the right way was to feed the baby calf."

Then she told Olympia the saddest truth. The baby calf with Olympia's eyes was dead and broken, drowned by the milk that they had fed him.

She could feel the shaking that started in Leah. It trembled up her legs and side. It was tiny at first, but then it became a quaking; a fragile earthquake next to her inside her friend's thin bones.

Olympia wrapped her arms around herself, trying to keep the shaking out of her own body where it bumped up next to Leah's.

56. Knowing

Leah kept shaking and talking.

"But I know something else, something really important."

Olympia waited while Leah took a huge shuddering breath, then she turned and took Olympia by the hand.

"I know what it means. It means that he was wrong. My dad didn't know how to feed a baby calf. He thought he remembered how to do it, but he didn't."

Leah squeezed Olympia's hand.

"And I know something else," she repeated.

Olympia felt the air around them get heavy, full of rain. The wind gusted around the bare trunks of the orange trees. Thunder pounded miles away.

When a flash of lightning stabbed through the gray sky, Olympia started to count, "One-one-thousand, two-one-thousand, three-one-thousand . . ." She got up to seven-one-thousand before the rumble of thunder stopped her. "My granny taught me how to count to know how far away the storms are. That storm is seven miles away."

Leah jumped up. Olympia was surprised.

"Listen to me, I need to tell you. My father didn't know what to do. He got it all wrong, and I think . . . he could be wrong about . . . other stuff, too. Maybe even your dad, too. Maybe all the dads; maybe there's stuff they don't remember right."

Olympia closed her eyes.

"Shhhh, I'm listening for the thunder."

"But did you hear me?"

Olympia kept her eyes closed and listened for thunder and thought about Leah's notion that dads might not know everything.

"I can hear you; you sound like thunder, but closer."

"Olympia, don't be mad at me. I didn't know. They told me what they know, and I thought I was supposed to know it too."

Leah dropped to her knees at the foot of the stairs. She looked up at Olympia, her green eyes full of wanting, her body tight and stiff.

Olympia leaned down and kissed her friend on the cheek. She thought about what she wanted to say.

She said, "Sometimes the king doesn't know everything. Remember, Leah? Sometimes the prince has to show him the right way, remember the story? Those cannibals, you know, like in the book. It could be like that. What do you think?"

Olympia watched the tightness pour out of Leah. She swayed a little like a palm frond in the rising breeze.

Lightning flashed again. This time when Olympia counted, Leah counted with her. When Olympia looked at Leah in surprise, she told her that her Grandmother Breck had taught her how to count the miles too. The thunder was farther away, one-one-thousand-and-ten, and that meant the storm was ten miles away—farther away, not closer. The storm wasn't coming for them.

Leah looked giddy with relief.

"I had forgotten about that king and his son," she said. "I think that it means . . . that we can do anything, think anything we want, if it's right and good or better."

"Sometimes they do know stuff. Like how to

count for lightning."

Leah's smile was back like a watery moon in the daytime. She jumped up and grabbed Olympia's hand, dragging her to her feet.

"Come and see our car-fort in the orange grove? If it's still there, I don't know. We could look for it together."

The girls caught a glimpse of Blarney dashing around the orange grove in one of his fits—yipping at imaginary terrors, stopping to chase his own tail when he heard the faint rumble of thunder.

The girls looked at each other. Olympia had an idea, ran up the stairs and into the house. "Just a minute, Leah." The soft boom of footsteps on the raised wooden floor followed Olympia through the tiny house. A few minutes later, she popped through the door with a brown grocery bag. Grabbing Leah's hand, she pulled her across the yard toward the orange grove.

"Come on. I'm going to put your hair up in braids."

Olympia paused and opened the bag for Leah. It was full of rubber bands, plastic barrettes, and hunks of yarn and ribbon.

"Like we're going to a party."

It felt perfect to Olympia to laugh all the way to the edge of the orange grove holding Leah's hand, going together to find out what had become of a fort made out of the bones of a Volkswagen Beetle Bug.

57. Too Close

Inside the house, an old woman listened to two smart girls running off to play.

Out of the kitchen window a sharp flash of lightning caught her eye; she counted the numbers slowly, like her own granny had taught her when she was a little girl. It was one of those useful things to know how to do: count those miles to the thunder, to know how far away the lightning might be—to know how far away the danger could be.

Granny Mac got to one-one-thousand-and-three when the thunder made the air and the ground tremble—only three miles away. Closer. The storm had turned with the wind and was moving west now.

She stepped out onto the wooden porch. The wind gusted. She wanted to believe that she could still smell salt and brine and the sharp tang of seaweed all the way from the Atlantic in the rain. She could have smelled all those things—once—when she was a young woman, growing up on the edges of other women's orange groves and celery fields.

Lightning flashed. She counted again, watching the smoke from the burn barrel shift. She'd only gotten to one-one-thousand-and-two, only two miles, when thunder rattled the ground under her feet.

Groaning, she limped to the bottom of the steps, hoping the girls had not wandered out of earshot. It seemed a long walk to get all the way across the backyard. The wind whipped smoke from the burn barrel into her lungs, making her double over. The coughing tore at her lungs.

At the edge of Miss Lockerbee's orange grove, Granny Mac put her hands to her mouth and tried to get enough air inside her to be able to call a warning to her granddaughter and the little white girl from over across the way.

58. Still the Same

It wasn't the worst thunderstorm that season, but it was the saddest. Blarney started running before anyone could hear the first clap of thunder. Bobby had been trying to find Leah when he saw the dog running in brainless circles. He tried to catch the big, red dog before he reached the orange grove, but Blarney was too frightened when a bolt of lightning jumped miles ahead of the storm like a warning sent from Mount Olympus. It raked through the air, searching, finally hitting one of the oldest orange trees in the center of the grove. When it hit the tree, there was an explosion of sparks. Fire spread through the orange grove, jumping from dead treetop to dead treetop. By the time the rain came, it was too late to save Miss Lockerbee's orange grove. The fire had burned so hot and so fast, the rain had made no difference.

The thunder and lightning hit Evegan at the same time that Blarney went stupid with fear. Leah's brother ran home, screaming for his mom to call the fire department.

It wasn't the worst thunderstorm of the season, but it drove Blarney the Irish setter off—forever. The dog started running; he never came back. Later, the kids at Evegan Elementary would say that the silly, red dog was probably still running—just ahead of the storm, maybe all the way to Tampa and then to the Gulf of Mexico, and then he'd jumped into the Gulf and kept right on swimming, probably to Texas.

Watching the orange grove burn and the volunteer firemen do what they could, Bobby's mother asked him the same questions over and over.

"Where's Leah? Do you know where your sister is?"

By the time the Evegan Volunteer Firefighters had arrived, the fire had spread to the edges of the five acres of damaged citrus, stopped by the sugar sand road that formed a lucky firebreak around the border. The piles of abandoned brush at the back of the orange grove turned into a wall of blistering heat.

Watching the firefighters, Bobby said, "I think she's at that girl's house; that girl, Olympia's house. You know, that colored girl in her class. That's the way she went. Will you be mad at her if she is over there?"

He watched his mother's hands start to shake as she held them against the sides of her face.

"No, I won't be mad."

It was luck that the fire burned itself out at the back edge of the orange grove before it jumped the dirt road into the woods. The heaps of brush left after the pruning had burned like napalm, a fire hot enough to reduce the world to its most basic parts— carbon, nitrogen, and hydrogen. Those forgotten piles of dried brush might have provided a perfect bridge for the fire to jump from the grove to the woods and then the ranch lands beyond, but it had burned too quickly and too hot and exhausted its fuel source. It was luck that the fire burned itself out so quickly. It was luck that it had burned so hot.

Later, in a tangled pile of illegally dumped junk, the VW Bug looked like the bones of a slaughtered bison, left blackened by a prairie fire. That was Chief Smithfield's first impression: that some farmer's bull or cow had been caught by the swiftness of the burning and trapped by the fire wall of destruction created by one lightning strike. He'd been walking the perimeter of the burn zone to make sure all the hot spots were out, or soon would be, when he found the VW Bug and the pile of junk. Kicking at the blackened bones of the car, he sighed as ash drifted over the inside of the wreck.

That's how he found them.

His next thought was that he was looking at lace, but it was a lace made of darkened bits of bone and ash. The fire had swept over them, leaving only the slender suggestion of two small bodies, the delicate remnants of their skulls close enough to have been touching once, cheek to cheek.

One of the rookie guys, a kid just back from Vietnam, found him staring at the burned-out pile of junk.

"Are there . . . two . . .," the rookie began, and then sighed. "The parents thought their girls were at the other one's house. Mrs. Breck said that her daughter left earlier, upset, and headed toward the colored girl's house, and Moody Crooms just got home from work to find the girl's grandmother collapsed, and his girl gone off. I talked to them both, Moody and Mrs. Breck. The Breck girl's father is out of town, something with that capsule fire out at the Cape. Hell of a thing to come home to. If it is the two . . ."

"Yeah, it's them," Smithfield said. "The old woman?"

"Stroke maybe." The rookie shrugged, dismissing the question.

"What about this? What do we say to the parents about finding them . . . like this?" the rookie wanted to know. When Smithfield didn't answer, he continued, "In Nam the parents were on the other side of the world, not waiting on the corner of Spring Hill and Old Town."

Smithfield hesitated, listening to the shifting and settling of ash, the random snap of the cooling ruins.

"We're going to tell them what we always tell people; there's been a tragic accident, an act of God, that kind of stuff. You'll get the feel for it."

The two men looked at the bodies lying side by side. It was hard to decide where one body ended and the other began.

"It's not like I haven't seen this kind of thing before, God knows. But without dog tags . . . ," the rookie mopped at his face, "how do you know?"

"Know what?"

"Which is which? You know, which one's the Breck girl and which one's Moody Croom's kid? You know . . . which one's white and which one's the colored kid? How can you tell?"

It was a stupid question; a rookie question. Smithfield thought about taking time to explain procedure, the coroner's job, the new techniques using dental records. Instead he squatted down, the way he would when he talked to a child, so he could be face to face. Looking at the two skulls, he realized they weren't much bigger than the size and shape of his curved hand—exactly the same.

Down here he could see the identical gaps in their teeth, the way the two girls had collapsed into each other, becoming a basket weaving of fragile, interlaced bone. The fire had covered the children in its single, indifferent blanket. Like God, he thought, it had been no respecter of persons, treating them the same.

"Can you tell?"

It was a stupid question—a rookie question.

"The same. Underneath, it's all the same.

Besides, it hardly matters anymore."

When the moon rose later that night, a last gust of wind kicked up a swirl of sparks that flew up into the blackness like tiny stars. It spiraled up from the heart of a derelict car chassis at the edge of what was left of Miss Lockerbee's orange grove.

59. *After*

When the world was new and orange trees grew wild, which is to say that the trees grew here or there or wherever and not in neat, straight lines the way people like to grow trees now, the people grew wild too, teaching their children the right ways to live and be happy. Those people taught their children that the tree of life was really an orange tree that lived forever—the same way everyone lives forever, even after they die. That's the way the people and the trees used to be.

They taught their children that when people died they went to live in a beautiful garden with grapes and apples and pomegranates and, of course, oranges. In the garden, they got to play games and be happy. One of the games they played was with the fruit from the orange trees. The people who had been old when they died played with oranges that were dried up and brown. The people who were in the middle of living when they died played with plump round oranges—perfectly ripe. The young ones, the children who died before they had ripened into grown-ups, played with small, green oranges.

When the world was new and orange trees grew wild, the people grew wild too, believing that their children lived forever even after they died, playing with oranges that were the wrong color.

ABOUT THE AUTHOR

 Linda Zern is a native Floridian where she learned to be moonstruck.

Mrs. Zern has published an inspirational book, The Long-Promised Song, serving as both writer and illustrator. Three collections of her humorous essays (ZippityZern's Uncommon Nonsense) can be found at Smashwords.com. Her award winning essays have been recognized and published at HumorPress.com.

Her current project, Mooncalf, is her first work of historical fiction for Middle School readers. Set in rural Central Florida, the author tells the story of two misfit girls and the hard lessons they must learn about friendship and love from their friends, their families, and their world.

The mystical state of Florida remains an enchanting and delightful place for both Mrs. Zern and her husband of thirty plus years, and so they continue to make their home among the palmettos and armadillos in the historic town of Saint Cloud.

Visit her website at www.zippityzerns.com

Made in the USA
Columbia, SC
08 December 2023

28106271R00098